I0549810

Northwest Vignettes

Volume Two

Creative Nonfiction Stories by NW Writers

Selected by

Eckley Guerin
and
Patricia Williams

Moonlight
Garden

Copyright 2018, Eckley Guerin.
All rights reserved.

Cover photograph by L. W. Moore.

Some story art by Diantha Weilepp,
Mick Alderman, Agnes Brown, Cat Loyd,
and Rennee Hammons.

Edited by Caitlyn Schmidt, Eckley Pat Guerin,
and S. C. Moore.

Published 2018, Moonlight Garden Publications,
an imprint of Gazebo Gardens Publishing, LLC.
www.GazeboGardensPublishing.com

978-1-938281-62-4   (paperback)
978-1-938281-63-1   (e-book)

Library of Congress Control Number: 2017915321

Printed in the United States of America.

ACKNOWLEDGEMENTS

We would like to thank all the many fine writers and illustrators who made this book possible.

Our staff of half a dozen volunteers, including Patricia Williams and Lorraine Andriesian, collected, organized, and typed up all the stories submitted for this collection and gathered illustrations.

Unfortunately, we had a run of bad luck. First, our very helpful courier, Bob Bohnke, moved out of state, then the remainder of our staff—either by accident or illness—left the project, until we were down to one volunteer, me.

Fortunately, Shelley C. Moore of Gazebo Gardens Publishing is the type of person who is willing to jump right in and offer assistance, advice, and information. We also share the same set of ethics and beliefs, so we work well together.

Luckily, I finally found three new volunteers to help me finish the project by reading through more story submissions, typing up stories, and creating illustrations: Jody Mumford, Rennee Hammons, and Cat Loyd. They helped me ready and send all the materials to Shelley, allowing our collection of short stories and illustrations to be published.

I'd also like to give a special thank you to LeRoy Moore for providing the photograph for the cover.

The royalties from the sale of this book will be donated to Clatsop Community Action in Astoria, Oregon, and the South Clatsop Country Food Bank in Seaside, Oregon.

Eckley Guerin

TABLE OF CONTENTS

In loving memory of the following
valued citizens of Clatsop County, Oregon:

Marge Bloomfield,
William Boone,
Wm. C. Elder,
Michel Foster,
Rae Goforth,
Brian F. Harrison,
Mitch Mitchum,
Carol Moore,
Walt Garnett,
and Hal Snow.

They will be missed.

"He was gasping and spitting water..."

Just Another Day at the Beach

Genessee Dennis

It had been about a month since I started lifeguarding at Imperial Beach in southern California. It was a typical SoCal day, sunny and warm.

The water conditions were fair. We were seeing the end of a big south swell. It was down to about six foot that day, but there was a mean long shore current because of it.

Long shore is when the current travels right along the beach, sometimes at great speeds and distances. At our beach, those were terrible conditions because we had a pier at one end of the beach and a jetty on the other that swimmers could be pushed into by such currents. We were always on our toes on days like these.

I was in Tower Four, the farthest north tower on the beach. Directly in front of me was the rock jetty—about fifty yards of just nasty jagged rocks. We had one red flag posted a good seventy-five yards south of the jetty. This was farther than usual but necessary because of the current pushing swiftly right into the jetty. We used the red flags to mark dangerous swimming areas. No one was allowed past that point.

Sitting in my tower, I noticed three boys bouncing along in the current. Bouncing was the term we used to describe a person in water depth barely able to touch ground—usually neck deep. Real touchy, because if they're bouncing along and hit a drop off, and they can't swim—gone, just like that!

I got up to make a P.A.—preventative action—on the loudspeaker. I spoke into the mike, telling the kids to stay south of the red flag.

I could tell they didn't hear me. I might have waited until they got closer, but they were moving so fast, it would have been too late. I radioed Pier Tower to advise them of the situation and asked that they send one of the mobile units over to make a P.A. on its loudspeaker.

The truck came over and made the P.A., telling the kids to come in and move south of the red flag. They began to comply, and the truck moved back into position in front of Tower Three, the next tower south of me.

The kids had moved, but not far enough. Soon, there they were again, heading past the flag. I called up Pier Tower, and they immediately ordered the truck over again.

Tensely watching the kids, I was wondering where the heck the truck was. I looked farther south and saw the truck having trouble getting through the crowd on the beach.

My heart began pounding as I realized I might have to go in after the kids. Then, two of them started coming in to shore, but the third—the smallest—couldn't touch bottom anymore. That's when I decided to go.

I threw off my shirt and grabbed my buoy and fins. As I jumped off the tower, I heard someone in Pier Tower yelling, "Somebody better get that kid!"

I had about fifty yards of running and swimming to reach the boy. By this time, he was only twenty-five yards away from the jetty and moving fast.

I ran up the beach, hit the water, dropped my rescue tube, and slung the harness over my shoulder. Not having much time, I swam right next to the jetty to try to intercept him. Finally, I reached him and grabbed his hand, just a couple of feet before he hit the rocks.

Heading south, I swam the boy away from the jetty and back to shore. He was gasping and spitting water, but he was alive and uninjured.

I walked him up to the truck to fill out an incident

report. He gave the other lifeguards his information.

Name: Billy
Age: eight
Weight: fifty pounds

He said, "Thank you," to me and then ran off into the crowd.

"Good job," the lifeguards in the truck told me.

"Just another day at the beach," I responded.

Genessee Dennis' father named him after the Genessee Mountains in New York. Gen is a quiet man, capable, responsible, and always aware of his surroundings. He was lifeguarding for the Astoria Aquatic Center when he wrote down this adventure. He had been in the Army and was in his early twenties when he guarded in Southern California. Gen, his wife, and their two sons now reside in Seaside, Oregon, where he is a firefighter.

"What if he'd escaped outside when someone had opened the door?"

Herman's Holiday in Paradise

N. Lee Chateau,
DVM—Animal Doctor

"Oh, no! Where's Herman? It's Christmas morning."

Mr. and Mrs. Miller had left Herman with us the day before for boarding over the Christmas holidays. They were going to spend the week in Southern California visiting relatives.

On their way out the door, I told them, "Don't worry, we'll take good care of him."

Herman was a nice hamster with long whiskers and a cute little nose. The Millers had presented Herman in a wire hamster cage with all his needs within, including a shiny exercise wheel.

"Where's Herman?"

He wasn't there! He was the last boarder to be served a special Christmas dinner that morning. The dogs and cats had been cared for and had eaten all their treats. Herman was in Ward 5 near the back of the animal hospital. Or rather, that's where he was supposed to be. That's where he had been when I left on Christmas Eve.

Rather than leave him cooped up in his confining cage, I had opened its door so he could play in the more open space of the upper kennel, which was about thirty inches cubed and had a screen door. I'd placed extra bedding out, found playthings for Christmas Eve, and left the ward door cracked open so he could watch the wall clock as the hands struck midnight, announcing the

4

start of Christmas morning. Now, Herman was gone—missing! Panic took my breath away.

"Wait!" I told myself. "I need to get a grip on things. I need to think logically. How did he escape? Where could he have gone?"

The only way he could have gotten out was at the bottom corner of the screen door of the upper kennel by the lower hinge, a space about one inch wide.

Very tight, but possible, I thought.

Below Herman's lair was a large kennel occupied by sweet Molly, a blonde golden retriever. Her folks had also gone away for the holidays, and Molly was staying with us. She had just finished the scrumptious Christmas dinner I had prepared specially for each of the furry critters in the house. She was curled up on thick blankets back in the corner of her kennel, satiated from her meal—warm and relaxed.

"Molly, you didn't!" I blurted out. "You didn't eat Herman, did you?"

Poor Molly instantaneously glanced up with guilt all over her face and cowered deeper into her blankets, trying to avoid eye contact.

Oh, no. Now what am I gonna do? went through my mind. *I know, I'll have to make Molly vomit. Then I'll know for sure if Herman left this world as part of Molly's Christmas dinner.*

A few minutes later, Molly was on the receiving end of an emetic I carefully administered by injection. A few minutes after—urp, gag, retch! Urp, gag, retch! Urp, gag, retch! Three times, and three neat piles.

I stroked Molly's head and praised her. "Good dog, Molly. Good dog."

Molly looked up at me with disdain and seemed to say, "I don't know what was good about that. Now I really feel sick."

Ten minutes! Ten minutes I spent teasing through Molly's dinner remains on the concrete floor—and no evidence of Herman.

He's not there—but wait. Maybe Molly had him for a Christmas Eve snack during the night. I led Molly off to the X-ray table and snapped two films. *Maybe I'll be able to see little hamster bones on the X-rays of Molly's insides—if she's guilty.*

A few minutes later, the films came out with perfectly normal findings. Molly was in the clear. Later, having given time for Molly's stomach to settle down, I served her another Christmas dinner with a tiny candy cane on top.

"Oh, Molly, I'm so sorry I accused you of eating Herman. Good dog, Molly, good dog," I said as I stroked her forehead.

She looked at the food, then she looked up at me out of the corner of her eye and seemed to say, "You're not trying to trick me, are you, doc? I don't want to go through that again."

I don't know if I will ever regain Molly's trust, because when she left a couple days later with her family, she only gave me a sideward glance as she quick-footed it out of the building.

Now the search was on in earnest. I scoured the animal hospital—looked in every nook and cranny, around and behind everything, on shelves, under and behind refrigerators, down the drain holes, and in the operating room, the dark room, the laboratory and exam rooms, offices and reception area, the bathroom, and even out in the dog runs with five-foot high concrete walls.

No Herman. He's gone! I checked the time on the clock. *Noon. Christmas day! I'd better get home to the family. We have company coming over for Christmas dinner.* My stomach was all knotted up. *But where could he be?*

I confess I was not very good company for our houseguests because my mind was fixated on one recycling question, *Where could Herman be?*

Christmas evening, I felt obligated to call the Millers in Southern California. They'd given me the number of Mrs. Miller's sister in Santa Ana where they planned to stay. I reluctantly phoned and heard a taped message telling me the family was out for the evening.

The next morning, I phoned again and got a message saying the whole family had gone to Disneyland. Not wanting to upset their holiday happiness, I chickened out and didn't leave a message. Besides, I felt the Millers should hear firsthand about Herman's fate instead of through recorded channels.

The following day, I did get up enough nerve to call again. Now, the message said that everyone had left for San Diego for the rest of the week. This time, I did leave our hospital number and a message.

"Mr. and Mrs. Miller, this is Dr. Chateau. This is important. I need to talk to you about your little Herman."

My staff and I spent the next two days looking everywhere in the hospital for any evidence of the little hamster. Nothing. Not a thing! No Herman.

Later, as I was leaving the hospital through the side door, my mind lit up. What if he'd escaped outside when someone had opened the door? I searched around the building, looking in the grassy areas. A shadow streaked across the ground. Glancing up, I saw a red-tailed hawk circling overhead.

Oh, no. What if Herman came out on the wrong side of a predator-prey relationship? Is Herman still out in the field, or is it already too late? After spending thirty minutes crisscrossing the grassy field and finding nothing, it became apparent. *It's time to give up and face reality. No more Herman!*

Just after closing time, a phone message came in. "This is Mrs. Miller. We'll be in on New Year's Eve to pick up Herman." Click.

I had to think through the options. It didn't seem right, proper, or ethical to go out and buy another hamster to replace Herman, or even to pay the cost of another hamster, since the new hamster would not be Herman. I'd just have to face the music. I'd need to see what the Millers wanted to do.

The next day after arriving at the hospital and starting morning rounds, I spotted some mouse pellets on top of the X-ray table.

Wait. We have never had a problem with rodents in the hospital building. Then, a light bulb flashed on in my logical left brain. *Hamster droppings...Herman's alive!*

Our staff spent every spare moment that day looking throughout the hospital again, pulling out drawers, looking under sinks, going through the filing cabinets, even pulling the refrigerators out and tipping them up to look into the compressors' machinery. Still no Herman.

The following morning—more hamster droppings on the X-ray table. Back by the table were storage shelves for dog food.

Aha! I found where a hole had been chewed in a dog food bag, and I deduced a hamster could have access to shallow water accumulating in the ward gutters.

We repeated our searching, this time taking each book out of the bookcase and going through every locker in the building. No Herman. Dang.

It was now the day before New Year's Eve, and I decided I should go back to the hospital at night with a flashlight. Maybe I could catch the reflection from a little hamster's eyes. That night, I tried this technique, shining the light around inside the hospital. Then, I heard loud pounding on the side door. I opened the door and was met with a bright light in my eyes.

The deputy from the Sheriff's Department said, "Oh, it's you, doc. I was out on patrol and thought maybe you were being burglarized."

I told him I was looking for a hamster, which had escaped from his kennel and was "on the lam." I don't know that he believed me.

After an hour, it was time to give up and go home. As a last resort, I moved some laboratory equipment and climbed up on a counter to shine the flashlight behind the fifty-five-gallon hot water heater. The four and a half foot high, round, upright electric water heater was strapped in the corner, tight against both walls. There was just the small triangular open space where the arc of the heater housing touched the two walls at a ninety-degree angle with one another. Barely enough space for even a closed fist.

Peering down the narrow channel, I spotted something under the light beam—a ball of fur on a white bed. "Herman! You're alive!" I confess I choked up and shed a few tears.

I noticed a cache of dog kibble tucked away in the corner of his bed. He had food, he had a warm hideaway, he had access to water—a Paradise on Earth. Herman stirred a little. He was now quite plump, kind of like the fat mouse, Gus, in Walt Disney's *Cinderella*.

How did he get behind there, and how can I get him out?

It would be a horrendous job to take out the laboratory cabinets to undo all the plumbing, wiring, and safety apparatus. We had no hand forceps long enough to reach Herman, and a hook on a line was not appropriate. There was less than one inch of clearance under the heater, so Herman could probably no longer get out on his own either.

Looking around the room, I saw the Shop-Vac and came up with a brilliant idea. I placed a narrow attachment to the tip of the vacuum hose and lowered it carefully down behind the heater until it was just above fat little Herman.

Is this going to work? My heart started pounding, my breath was paralyzed, and my muscles tensed in anticipation. I hit the ON switch.

"Hang loose, little guy. Elevator, going up!"

The suction was working. Carefully and cautiously, I retrieved the very fat little Herman, hustled him quickly to his own hamster cage, and closed him in.

"Whew!" I breathed a sigh of relief after a week of anguish.

Next, I vacuumed up his custom bed and discovered he had made it out of laundry lint and cotton. I transferred his fine bed to his cage so he could rest in comfort for another night. I later discovered he had raided a bag of cotton balls from a shelf and teased apart some of the balls to use as his mattress. What an industrious and ingenious guy!

That night, before I left the wards, I stopped by to make sure he was okay. I commented, "Herman, it might be a good idea if you started working out on your exercise wheel before you hit the sack."

Herman looked me straight in the eyes and wiggled his nose. "Climb way up that wheel? Fat chance," he seemed to say, and he snuggled into his fluffy bed, XXX enlarged!

Late in the afternoon on New Year's Eve, my receptionist called back in a pleasant voice, "Doctor, the Millers are here for Herman."

I carried Herman up to the front in his cage.

Mr. Miller said, "You wanted to tell us something about Herman."

I started, "Well, Mr. and Mrs. Miller, I'm afraid Herman put on a little weight while..."

That set off a resounding duet of chuckles, "Ha, ha, hee, hee, ha, ha."

At once, without hesitation, Mr. Miller picked up Herman in his cage, and they headed for the door. "Thanks, doc. We'll put him on a diet, but now we have to get to a New Year's Eve party."

They were gone in an instant, and I was left standing there with an open mouth and a mind ready to spill untold secrets.

I phoned the Millers on the afternoon of New Year's Day and finally told them the rest of the story. And, as that well-known saying goes, "All's well that ends well."

N. Lee Chateau is the pen name of a retired Doctor of Veterinary Medicine residing on the North Oregon Coast. He volunteers at the Clatsop County Animal Shelter and Columbia Memorial Hospital. He and his wife now enjoy traveling to visit their children and grandchildren.

"During the shipwreck, I was not scared."

All for Twenty-Five Dollars

Dora Bigelow Gearhart
adapted from her journals

Johnny heard the rattling of oats in the pan. He nickered and came trotting. I thought he suspected I held a rope halter behind my back, but the oats were such a delicious treat that he didn't care. Besides, he knew I weighed less than anyone else who ever wanted to ride him. Even my sister, Ella, whose horse he really was, weighed more. As he carefully mouthed up the last of the oats, I slipped the halter around Johnny's neck and led him to my brother, Newt, to saddle and ready him for our thirty-five mile ride to Myrtle Point, Oregon.

We lived in the post office compound of Eckley, above Powers, Oregon, and I was going to the 1905 Lewis and Clark Fair in that far off big city of Portland. This was my reward for taking care of the house, the garden, and the children when, after their hay was all in the barn, Ella and her husband, Harry Guerin, went to the Lewis and Clark Fair in late July.

Newt, living two and three-fourths miles away at our family home in Deer Park, was helping Father get the hay in there. Each evening, he rode horseback to see we were all right and stay all night with us, arriving at bedtime and leaving at four the next morning.

I had carefully cared for my niece and her brother, who helped me milk the cows, churn the butter, and can the fruit. I even canned several pints of peas, and they sealed and kept. Sister would be surprised. My nephew could be a caution, but Harry had him promise to behave, and he did—mostly.

Now, it was late August, and I had just turned sixteen years old. Harry gave me $25, and I was to go to the fair with Anna and Tom Guerin. Tom was Harry's brother. I would ride with the mail carrier, George, who was another of the Guerin boys—there were eight of them. We would stay at the Guerin Hotel in Myrtle Point where Tom and his father were the proprietors.

It was gossiped that the sheets were changed only once a week, as is true in some of the less fastidious establishments. But the Guerin Hotel changed its sheets after each room occupant checked out.

It was late when we got there. The beds all being full, I was put with Inez Lusk, a school teacher whose father and brother had stayed with us in Eckley many times.

After a good breakfast the Chinese cook had made, we left the next morning at 7:30 a.m. for Roseburg, Oregon, in the stagecoach drawn by four horses. The driver sat in the high seat in front, shared with Miss Huling and an old maid friend of hers from the East. It was the most comfortable seat and missed some of the dust. Anna, Tom, and I shared the second seat. The two men in the third seat caught the worst dust.

The morning was quite pleasant. At Remote, about fifteen miles to the east, the horses were changed, and again at Camas Valley, to keep the teams fresh and able to travel. At a clear, cool little stream gushing out of the mountains, we ate lunch. We had sandwiches, and Miss Huling shared a small suitcase full of lunch cupcakes and all kinds of goodies. I was amazed, as I had never seen such a lavish lunch.

Before we got over the mountains, a suspension spring broke. While changing horses at Camas Valley, the driver had it mended. Stagecoach drivers have a real rivalry going as to who is the most knowledgeable and efficient. Our driver had us hide behind a building while the incoming stage passed so the breakdown would not be detected.

The sun got hotter and the dust thicker as we traveled on. It was a quiet day with no wind to carry the dust away, and it rolled up in clouds, settling onto us in the second and third seats, choking us. Our faces were caked with it. Breast lamps were fastened onto the lead horses the last few miles to show the road.

We were a hungry, tired lot of people by the time we got to the Pioneer Hotel in Roseburg. The one pitcher of water provided for the three of us was scant washing for such dust. But afterwards, we ate and soon slept.

Next morning, we started on the Southern Pacific train north to Portland. The day was hot and the stops numerous. After over a hundred miles, and late in the evening, we finally arrived at the downtown depot.

Soon, my wondering eyes beheld the lights of Broadway. There were clusters of electric lights on the top of lampposts at stated intervals—a most beautiful sight that extended for several blocks. We took a street car on a thrilling ride out to the home of Lulu Walker Reynolds—who had lived in Myrtle Point for many years—where we were going to stay.

The Lewis and Clark Fair—such wonders! The amusement section, The Trail, was filled with all kinds of astonishments. I remember the horse that could count, the diving elk, and the trained seals. In the Alaska exhibit, the big gold nugget inside a wire cage took my eye. By grasping it firmly, I could just flop the cage over. It was that heavy. There were beautiful flower arrangements at the park and many animals. I had always heard of the cute monkeys. Well, I thought a lot of the things they did were anything but cute. They scratched a lot and threw anything at hand.

One day, we took an excursion boat to the Cascade Locks and back. I hadn't brought my winter coat. I just about froze, as it was very cold on the Columbia River. And it had been so hot in the city.

Finally, it was time for me to take *The Kilburn* down the Columbia River to start south for Coos Bay, on the way home to Myrtle Point, and finally back to Eckley. I took a streetcar down to the dock late one evening and was fortunate to get into a cabin with Mrs. Ella Knapp, and her young son, of Port Orford, Oregon. We went right to bed.

I woke up early to see the sights as we approached Astoria at the mouth of the Columbia River. We were following the Great River of the West Trail of Lewis and Clark. Next thing, we were going over the Columbia Bar, one of the roughest and most dangerous systems of bars and shoals in the world.

The captain looked at me and told me that I was getting pale and had better go to bed. That was before breakfast, and I became awfully sick. I was sick all day.

Along about 2:00 a.m. the next morning, I awoke. Mrs. Knapp, who lived by the ocean and had made many ocean voyages, was standing by the window. I asked her if anything was wrong.

She said, "I hear breakers!"

It was foggy and dark. We began to pitch around some—went up and came down onto something hard. We did that three times and then stayed still. We had been tossed onto the South Jetty at the entrance of Coos Bay. The rudder was out of commission, and we drifted onto a sand spit.

After the first crash, we were ordered to dress and get on our life preservers. Under our bunks, we found some—old ones with no straps to fasten them together. We put them on anyway and went up on deck. I noticed some men whom we had seen the day before with their wives, and I had thought at the time, *What devoted couples.* These men were now alone. Finally, their wives, white as sheets, barely able to stand, came crawling onto deck. My picture of devoted husbands changed.

Thank the Lord, the weather was calm. Coffee was brought on deck for all, and it was strong enough to stand alone. I was really very well, considering I had eaten nothing since boarding the boat and had tried to throw up all the day before. Finally, about 8:30 a.m., the tide lifted us off the sand spit. A tug towed us to North

Bend, where a launch took us to the town of Marshfield, renamed Coos Bay in 1946. On the launch was Frona Summerlin, just going home. I thought she was the prettiest person I had ever seen.

As we were being towed, *The Kilburn* listed to one side considerably. Looking over the railing, I could see splintered boards under the water. We had sunk about four foot above the water line in just that short distance with all the pumps going. It was noon when we got to Marshfield, and I hurried to the Blanco Hotel to get something to eat.

On my way to the dining room, who should come up behind me but my brother, Wells. He had heard of the wreck when in Myrtle Point, so he got on the train and came to see if I was all right. During the shipwreck, I was not scared—I felt very capable and sufficient. If I were drowned, that was that. I was a little surprised to find my brother looking for me.

As I had planned to visit with Edith Kelsey for overnight, Wells went right back to Myrtle Point on the train without me. A rowboat took me across the bay to Eastside where Edith lived.

The next day, I took the train to Myrtle Point and then met Johnny at the livery stable. He nickered to show how glad he was to see me. I rode with the mail carrier back to Eckley, having seen the big city, the Lewis and Clark Fair, and been in a shipwreck—all for $25.

Dora Bigelow Gearhart was born in 1888. A year after her trip to the Lewis and Clark Fair, she graduated from Myrtle Point High School and obtained a position at Dora School in the Pleasant Hill District. Dora was married in 1909. She and her husband had two daughters and three sons. Besides raising the children, Dora was busy with gardening, sewing most of the family's clothes, maintaining a flourishing orchard, and never-ending washing on a scrub board with water from the well heated in a copper boiler on the wood stove. She passed in 1978, aged a month less than ninety.

"...any kind of paying job was scarce."

The Great Depression

Berdena M. Nichols

We didn't call them panhandlers back in those years. We called them hoboes. They didn't live on city streets and ask for money. They didn't sleep on downtown sidewalks. They followed railroad tracks and knocked at doors, asking the lady of the house if she could spare a cup of coffee or a piece of bread.

They sat around a bonfire at the end of town in what we called hobo camps. They were men who rode in boxcars from town to town, searching for work to earn a dollar to send home.

I know, because I remember those years from 1926 to 1936. I saw hoboes split wood in return for a cup of hot coffee and a slice of Mama's bread. I was seven years old, and Mama told me she could not turn someone hungry away. But finally, a day came when I did hear Mama turn a hobo away from our door.

"I cannot take food away from my children," she told him.

It had been a long while since anyone in town had heard the callboy—a man who called out train crews—jump off his bicycle and call out an engine's number. There was no work on the Southern Pacific Railroad for a young locomotive fireman with a family of five children, like my daddy—or for anyone else, either. So, we drove away from our comfortable grey house through sleepy little towns until we stopped in a small southern Oregon town. Grandma opened her door to us.

Life went on. The sun still rose in the morning and sank in the evening. School bells rang.

Though there were no jobs for the men to leave the house for, the women had much housework to get done. Parsnips and carrots left in the ground in Grandma's garden that winter became very precious, as did every nickel in Daddy's pocket. Mama watered down already-diluted milk.

When emptied of flour, sugar, and salt, the cotton bags they came in, which we called sacks, hung bleaching on the clothesline. We were not ashamed to wear clothes made from them, and we watched Daddy cut and glue stick-on soles to our worn out shoes. We carried penny pencils and nickel tablets to school. Penny postcards arrived in the mail.

I saw Daddy dig ditches in the rain for the Works Progress Administration, or "Make Work," as many shamed workers called it.

I told Daddy, "I saw some men just lean on a shovel and roll cigarettes."

Daddy grinned and responded, "That, I've observed."

Ten dollars a month for house rent was a lot of money on about $40 a month income. Daddy told us if we were going to survive, we had to get out of town.

We gathered about the table and listened as Daddy explained to us the offer made to him by a man who had an old farm with pastured beef cattle up in the hills, deserted for many years.

"Rent free, no water or light bills, no wood to pay for," Daddy told us. "There's ground to plant all the gardens we want and fruit for the picking. It means lots of work: fences to be repaired, garden ground to be plowed, and an outhouse to be moved. We'll have to draw up our water from the well—no pump. And you kids will have a three-mile walk through the hills to a one-room school."

Five big-eyed kids all shouted, "Goody!"

The day we moved to our home in the hills was not one to be forgotten. Long, straight rows of green plants—their crooked necks poking up out of the damp brown earth—greeted us.

The sun had come out after an Oregon rain, leaving the weathered, rough boards on the barn, the house, the woodshed, and the outhouse steaming in the warm sunshine. Long-neglected, gnarled, fruit trees were beautiful, covered in pink and white blossoms and filled with buzzing bees.

At first sight, I fell in love with our home up in the hills. Daddy had gone there before school let out and repaired fences and planted a huge garden. Don't ask me where the seeds came from. I never asked. I only know there was every vegetable that grows under the sun planted there.

We sat on the barnyard fence watching our Jersey cow lazily chewing her cud. Daddy had done some work for a nearby farmer in exchange for her, the use of a plow, and a team of horses to plow the ground with.

We heard no echoes of lonely train whistles throughout the hills, but Daddy wasn't spoofing when he told us we'd hear coyotes howling. We jumped in fright at sight of one standing along the chuck-holed wagon trail on our two-mile walk to the mailbox.

Deer often leapt out in front of us, and we begged Mama and Daddy to be allowed to keep a spotted fawn as a pet, but they said, "Absolutely not!"

Although our furniture consisted of only the bare necessities, Mama's home-baked bread and crocheted rag rugs over the freshly scrubbed floors made the old four-room, unpainted house feel like a palace.

Our mother was a very thrifty woman. She could rip up, wash, and iron used and worn clothing and turn them into something we kids were proud to wear. She taught us to bake bread, churn butter, make cottage cheese, and heat the heavy, sad iron on top of the stove to iron our clothes.

We made starch with flour and boiling water, and it

fell upon me to cook the starch on washdays, if there was enough flour. One time, I plunged Sister's flour-sack unmentionables in the hot, thick starch—purposely. They stood on their own when dry. I laughed, but Sister didn't.

Mama, very soberly, stated, "Such a shame to waste so much flour."

Mama's favorite saying was often repeated. "Wasteful ways make wishful days that I may live to say, 'How I wish I had the crust of bread that once I threw away.'"

Mama always said there was no excuse to be dirty or wear clothes with holes in them. We brushed our teeth with baking soda, and we were scrubbed in the washtub with homemade lye soap.

In our little home in the hills, we had both good times and bad. Good times, like when we listened to Mama and Daddy sing together, when they told stories told to them by their grandparents about crossing the plains, and when they shared stories of the early pioneer days in Oregon. And bad times, like when I cried with a toothache.

There were days I knew I didn't deserve the sweet smiles my mother smiled upon me, and special times when she'd say, "Hold out your hand, Dena," on her return from the garden. She'd leave a little green frog to keep me company until it hopped away into the tall grass.

We five kids joined eight other kids in the little schoolhouse. Each day before the doors opened, my older brother built the fire so we could all dry out our wet coats and shoes. We pumped the well water we drank, and we raised our hands to ask permission to run to the outhouse. Our teacher read out loud while we ate cold lunches, and she never gave us homework to do after school hours.

There was one time we had cause to feel insecure, when Daddy was forced to make a tough decision. Should he accept a night job, which required him to leave our home and work in town? Should he leave Mama, with us five kids and the responsibility of the cattle and the garden, alone up in the hills? He would be unable to get home each weekend—but any kind of paying job was scarce. We sat down together, and he asked all of us what we thought he should do.

"How much will they pay, Dad?" my thirteen-year-old Brother asked.

"Four dollars a night."

"Whew! Then you'd better go, Dad!"

Daddy laid one hand over Mama's. She smiled. "Glen, the children and I will get along the best we know how. We will have to believe the good Lord will not allow any forest fires—or the cattle to break through the fences."

That settled the question.

Daddy told us it takes an engine, the cars, and the caboose to make up a train, and it takes both parents and all the kids pulling together to make a home. And push and pull we did. We all worked long, hard days and slept each night behind unlocked doors, and our garden flourished under Mama's loving care.

One time when he got a couple days off, Daddy took us, with a carload of vegetables, to visit friends in town. When our friends opened their door and saw all the green, red, and yellow vegetables, they cried. They had been eating boiled macaroni for a whole week.

On our way home, Mama asked us if we would like to move back into town. There was a loud chorus of, "NOOO!"

I learned a lifestyle throughout those long Depression years that I find difficult to forget. I still like to bake bread and darn socks, and I still like little green frogs and buzzing bees.

I hear people say, "I can't understand how on earth you survived such a life. I couldn't."

I smile. I know how we survived those Depression years before Daddy was called back to work as a locomotive engineer for the Southern Pacific Railroad

Company. The good earth took care of us—along with Daddy and Mama's help.

I would love to go back to our old home up in the hills someday. I would like to walk through wooded hills to the schoolhouse again. I am thirsty for a dipper of cold well water. I'd like to watch the bees fly in and out of pear blossoms.

Brother laughs when I speak of it and says, "Oh, Sis, you'd never know you were there if you did go. It's all paved streets and expensive houses now!"

I want to cry out to the homeless people of today—to all parents with hungry children—"Go to the hills!"

But where can they go? Most of the hills are already developed.

I once read, "When man despoils a work of man, we call him a vandal. When man despoils a work of nature, we call him a developer."

Exactly!

"I realized I couldn't live both lives."

Mellow in Mist

Kyle McCarthy

My mom loves to dance. The doctors told her not to, on account of her pregnancy, but she went ahead and danced anyway. One night, she went out to a dance with my dad, and I'm sure they had a great time, but a few hours later, in the early morning, there I was. It was April 12, 1987.

I was raised in the small town of Delavan, Wisconsin, and spent the first twenty-two years of my life there. My childhood was a classic Midwestern one, enjoying the lakes, streams, and camping trips to the northern woods, collecting lightning bugs in jars and giving them sticks and leaves for a home, hiking through the moraine landscapes in the south, trips to Lake Michigan and Milwaukee's lakefront, train rides to Chicago, where my dad was raised, and getting Chicago dogs and old fashioned sodas.

I always worked various minimum wage jobs but never stuck around at one job too long. I studied Graphic Design at the local technical college but never finished the degree.

In 2008, I was working third shift at a large resort, doing paperwork and minding the front desk. I had a little apartment, and a girlfriend. I had lots of friends and lots of acquaintances. We went out, ordered furniture from a website, clipped coupons, and shopped at Target. We had a puggle named Sophie. We'd walk Sophie around town, get Subway, go sit in the grass by the lake, and eat our submarine sandwiches. We'd go to our friend's houses for beer pong or Holiday parties.

It was my home, minutes from where I was raised. I knew everyone. I bought things. I was young. I was careless.

Somewhere along the way, the third shift hours were starting to wear on me, and I wasn't getting very much sleep. My girlfriend and I started to argue a lot. I was troubled when I thought of the state of the world and the nature of things. I felt sorry for a generation working their lives away, dreaming of a perfect retirement that would never come because they would die in debt before it was ever a possibility. I wondered what I should be doing and what the point of doing that was. I didn't want to live like a vampire anymore. I didn't want to eat instant ramen anymore.

As the months went on, and winter came creeping closer, I started to resent it all. I resented the status quo—which manifested itself in everything around me. My little town was the status quo. TV dinners were the status quo. Cell phones that we'd throw away every year for the next, newest model were the status quo. I felt like I was behind four inches of glass.

My girlfriend eventually left, and she took the Internet furniture and the puggle. I had a futon and a card table. I had no appliances and no TV.

There was a liquor store across the street from my apartment, and they had a discount rack. I would get off work, come home, try and write something, and drink scotch on the rocks. I don't really remember eating anything. I had a furnace that I couldn't afford to use— and it was so cold.

Some mornings, my fellow night shift workers and I would go out to this little bar. Those were good hours. Precious hours, as the sun rose and bedtime edged closer, having a few drinks with my coworkers at 7:00 a.m. in the morning. About 10:00 a.m., I would crash on the futon and sleep until 4:00 p.m. or 5:00 p.m. in the evening.

One morning, I arrived at my apartment after the night shift. It had snowed heavily overnight. It was thick. I remember how cold it was—unbelievably cold—somewhere below zero. It felt like being more naked than you've ever been—like bones in the wind.

When it snowed, the city would plow all the streets, but not the alleys. My alley was impassable. I couldn't park on the street or they would tow my car. I had to get to my garage. I was wearing dress shoes and a stunningly uncomfortable, Chinese-made, cotton and polyester suit. I had a little foldable shovel in my trunk, and I started to dig. I probably had frozen snot around the edges of my nose, and snow crusting my suit, but I was too cold to remember.

Two and a half hours later, I drove my car down the alley to my garage. I pulled in, went inside, and quickly fell asleep for the rest of the day. I didn't even have a drink. I had really hit a dead end.

In the spring, I decided to move back in with my mom and dad and sort things out. My dad came and helped me move the futon and table.

I kept working at the resort, commuting from my parents' house. I didn't want to spend time at home. I was always gone.

As the fresh and floral spring turned to the heady days of summer, I hung out with my friends more often. I sometimes went without sleep to hang out with them during their normal time-off hours. I was casually dating. I was having fun. We had bonfires, we partied, we drank. It was good enough for a while.

Still, I couldn't shake my discomfort with the existing state of affairs. I was bothered doing little things, like driving around during the day to do necessary errands when I was tired. When you work at night, it's actually uncomfortably bright at noon. It hurts your eyes. If I was feeling better about anything, it was due to the warmth of summer and my slipping into nihilism.

Finally, I'd just had it. I was done with my town. I didn't want a job that continually stole me away in the night. I didn't want to wear a nametag anymore, and I never wanted to shovel that much snow, ever again. I wanted to move away—far, far, away.

It was July 2009. The presidential campaign was getting insane. Wars were ongoing. I had to get out into the world. I had to get moving.

This is a massive nation, which sprawls over thousands of miles. I looked at a US map, and it was overwhelming. How did you choose to move somewhere? The South? No. Not Florida. Not New York or Los Angeles. I wasn't interested in the East Coast. Too cold. Too busy. Southwest? Too dry. I wanted a nicer climate, more agreeable people, and wilderness. I wanted to get lost.

Then it came to me—the Pacific Northwest. I started a massive online research process. I read everything I could, including travel guides, and watched TV shows and YouTube videos. And there it was, waiting for me. Oregon. It looked like one of the coolest places to be. There was so much going on! It was the opposite of every city in the Midwest.

Oregon was pulling at me, drawing me, calling me closer. Oregon was the refuge for washed up gold diggers, opportunists, retired soldiers, old sailors, explorers, loggers, captains, leftists, cooks, ranchers, hippies, hikers, hunters, bikers, and tattoo artists. It felt like the alternative melting pot of America.

My only previous experience with Oregon was playing *The Oregon Trail* game on my computer. Ford the river? Peter has dysentery. You've lost cattle. Mary ran away with an Indian. I didn't know anything about Oregon.

Suddenly, I realized there was this seemingly wild and far-flung place at the other side of the country. I wanted to see this new land. I wanted to explore. I wanted to struggle. I wanted to find meaning in something.

I needed help. I needed to do some research, look at apartments, find a job. I browsed listings all over

Portland, mostly looking for more front desk work, figuring I should go with my experience, try to scrape some money together, and then I could leave the night shift behind. I looked at pages and pages of listings, all in places I'd never heard of. I applied over and over and over. I didn't know if I was going about things backwards or not. I didn't know what I was doing.

I never heard back from anyplace. They probably wondered why some kid was applying for a job from 2,000 miles away.

I might have ended up in Portland, and maybe I would have loved it, maybe I would've bought a bike and lazed around the bookstores and hipster enclaves. But two roads emerged, and I took the other.

One day, I was browsing jobs in the Portland area, and I noticed an ad. It was odd. It didn't seem right. It was titled, "Mellow Country Life." I was overwhelmed with curiosity. The ad was posted in the jobs section of the biggest city in Oregon. Mellow country life? I clicked.

The farmer described himself as an older guy living on a homestead in a tiny community, an hour and half from Portland, called Mist. He had two daughters and a dozen chickens, and he planned to raise sheep. His ad was asking for help. It was hard for him to finish all the chores and repairs around the farm that constantly had to be done. He was looking for someone to stay on the property, to look after things, to put in a good day's work each day and to generally help out—a farm hand. In exchange, he offered room and board. There would be no money involved.

I'd never worked on a farm before. I'd never seen a live chicken. I'd never lived in the country. I was a city boy. I was young and naïve, and I wanted this more than anything. I replied. The farmer later told me that about thirty others had replied to his ad, but that in my email, he sensed an eagerness to learn and a willingness and the grit to put in a good day of work. I was hired.

When I told my parents that I'd made arrangements

to move away, they said it was rather sudden. I think my mom was heartbroken. It was only weeks away. It was easier for me that way. I didn't tell anybody much of anything.

I put in my two-weeks' notice at work. I packed my car with everything I owned—clothes, books, a computer, and a guitar. I bought a road atlas at Walmart. I didn't have a cell phone. I left Wisconsin on a quiet, sunny, September morning. I watched the house I grew up in disappear, then my street, then my neighborhood, then my city—and I was on the open highway.

My journey from the upper Midwest to northwestern Oregon would take me 2,100 miles. Southern Wisconsin is a gently rolling landscape with towns and cities scattered regularly along straight roads, studded between fields of golden corn and pastures of dairy cattle like cloves stuck into an orange.

I headed north and west toward the Mississippi and followed the Minnesota border toward the Twin Cities. Gradually, Wisconsin's landscape began to change as I drove farther north. Deciduous stands became coniferous forests, and the towns began to spread farther apart. I made my way along easily enough, and within my home state, it only felt like a vacation—like some extended road trip. It wasn't like moving away. But I was.

When I thought of what was to come, I experienced a new phenomenon. Where before, images of the daily grind would materialize, now I could see nothing at all. I was literally seeing myself driving into some great blackness—a void where there was no past and there was no future. Any outcome could result, and I struggled with not knowing how much power I possessed to control it. I was flung out into the space of the world. I was free.

I called my dad. He was at work, but he took my call. He sounded sad over the phone. He couldn't believe what I was doing, and neither could I.

It wasn't my intention to hurt my parents. I was just

going out and trying to discover something new. Maybe when you're in your early twenties, you simply don't consider thoroughly how your actions will affect the people around you. Perhaps we never consider them as much as we ought to.

My dad told me some comforting words, despite his discomfort with the situation—he did possess a certain stoicism. He reminded me that he was proud of me and that I was striving.

When I neared the Twin Cities of Minneapolis and Saint Paul, the traffic was getting heavy, and I was feeling tired, but I wanted to get through them. I hoped to at least get to Fargo by nightfall. From the Twin Cities, the heavy traffic faded away, and I drove into rural Minnesota. Heading westbound on Interstate 94, I saw many lakes in the area. There were small towns, and coniferous forests, and the still familiar feeling in the air.

By the time I reached the outskirts of Fargo, North Dakota, I'd driven almost 600 miles, and the light was fading. I found a Motel 8, picked up some beer, and ordered a pizza. I slept really well. The motto of Fargo is "The Gateway to the West," which I came to understand. The surroundings had begun to change.

From the vast Chippewa National Forest around I-94 in Minnesota, the land spread out and began to roll in long, low stretches. The interstate straightened and ran through oceans of crop fields with whole hillsides the green or gold of corn and wheat. Then there were miles and miles and miles of straight, wide-open countryside.

When I pulled off at a rest stop, I scraped layers of bugs off the entire front end of my car. A thousand tiny insect corpses must have collected there. I can only imagine the daily toll on the insect population of North Dakota in that vicinity. The traffic flowed by like a river. Massive semis were barreling down the straightaways.

To the west, I reached the badlands of Theodore Roosevelt National Park. It was an awesome sight. The great grass prairies rolled away to the horizon. The painted canyons were otherworldly and impressively striking with their multicolored strata. I saw horses there, as well as buffalo—wild creatures calling to mind ancient pre-Columbian times.

Montana is perhaps the most beautiful place I have ever seen. The sky is seemingly bigger than other places, as if they'd lifted the very dome of the heavens and widened it to accommodate more stars. "Big Sky Country" indeed!

I reached the city of Bozeman and found a campground on the outskirts, south of the city proper. I didn't have a tent, and they let me have a site for only a couple bucks after I told them what I was doing. I bought a couple bundles of wood, built a fire, and watched the moon rise over a ridge.

The next morning, I heard other campers saying the interstate was closed ahead into the mountains—a forest fire. I confirmed this with the campground staff and set myself down to consult the atlas. The alternate routes were hours and hours apart, and heading opposite directions. I chose to wait out the situation. Fortunately, just a few hours passed before the interstate was opened again, and I was on my way.

My first sight of the ravages of a forest fire became apparent as I progressed. I passed through an area that was entirely burned on both sides of the road. The ground was black. Charred stumps were smoking, and the air was hazy. Traffic was moving slowly through. To me, it seemed hellish, but forest fires, of course, are a part of the natural cycle of nature, and that particular one wasn't very large.

After a few miles, I found myself heading into the mountains, flanked by lush forests. The pace of traffic picked up, and soon enough, we were flying through mountain passes, gaining elevation, and then dipping again, rising and falling, and cornering at high speed, which, frankly, terrified me. But I was keeping up with the flow.

When I came out of the mountains, I came upon Idaho's Lake Coeur d'Alene, and it was a beautiful, shimmering sight. It was late afternoon. I considered stopping overnight again, but I was getting so close to my destination that I only stopped for a quick meal and continued on I-90 into Washington State.

It was there that the great national interstate highway I'd travelled to cross the country and I took our separate ways. I veered southwest through Spokane and burned through the 130 or so miles to Pasco, Washington. There before me was the mighty Columbia River. It was our first encounter, though it would not be our last.

I followed Highway 395 to Highway 82, and crossed the Columbia for a second time. Just like that—I was in Oregon. It was getting late, 10:00 p.m. or so, but there was no stopping. I wanted to make it to Portland and stop over there before continuing on to Mist.

What I remember of that part of Oregon is that it was like a wide-open prairie. It may have just been the night, but there wasn't much around. The gently rolling hills were a deep blue, and the night was cool.

I stopped for gas somewhere and reached for the pump, when a man appeared and hollered, "Stop! That's illegal."

I hadn't realized you couldn't pump your own gas in Oregon. He filled the tank for me, and I was on my way again. I realized later that I'd driven through a beautiful length of highway heading west to Portland, including the Columbia Gorge, but I couldn't see much in the dark.

Sometime around midnight, I arrived in Portland, Oregon. I passed underneath the welcome sign. It started to rain immediately.

There I was. I had made it so far on my own. My friends, my family, everything I'd known, was over 2,000 miles behind me. Had I made the right decision? Would it work out? Would the great new state swallow me whole? Would it spit me out?

I stayed in Portland for a few days. I couldn't just pass it by. I did the tourist thing. I got a Voodoo

Doughnut. It wasn't very good. I got lost in Powell's Bookstore. It was an incredible, exciting city, but I had to keep moving. I had a job to get to.

I drove through Portland's western suburbs, through the scenic, pastoral northern Willamette Valley, and into the hills and forests of the Coast Range. Highway 47 took me away from Highway 26—the Sunset Highway—and through the small town of Vernonia. I kept driving, passing over the curling waters of the Nehalem River several times. Farther and farther west, into the countryside, past the street lights, past the gas stations and grocery stores—then, sometime in the afternoon, on September 6th, 2009, I drove into the tiny, unincorporated community of Mist, Oregon.

I was lucky to find the right road, and I turned onto a long, graveled surface toward the homestead that would be my new home. I matched the address on the mailbox and pulled up.

Waiting there, with arms waving and a big smile on his face, was the farmer. He remarked that he was glad I was driving a Chevy, because he didn't like to work on Fords. We shook hands, and I got a chance to look around.

It was a large farm between a stretch of forest and the Nehalem River. It was absolutely beautiful! I saw chickens all over the place, and I got all worked up and eagerly pointed and laughed.

"Yep," the farmer said. "Them's the chickens."

He let me rest up for a few days before we got to work, but soon enough, the work began. I got roused about 6:00 a.m. in the morning and got a home-cooked breakfast, courtesy of the farmer or his daughters, and a hot cup of coffee before I headed out around the property.

For several weeks, he simply taught me everything he could. He taught me about the chickens, about their schedule, their diet, their laying habits. He showed me the vegetable garden, told me about the weeds, the watering, the planting routine, and the harvesting that we would soon be doing. He taught me how the water system worked, where the lines ran, and how to use the gas-powered pump to get water from the river, in case it didn't rain for a while. I made plenty of pots of coffee with Nehalem River water.

The farmhouse had no well, no city water to be found. We collected rainwater in separate five-gallon tanks and filtered it before it got pumped into the house. There was an extra canoe that we could put in the yard to hold more of the rainwater if needed, which meant that at any given time, with enough rain, which was usually very plentiful, we had over 1,000 gallons of water on hand—for free.

That was how the first several months went. I got up early, got fed a hearty breakfast, and got to my routine. I checked on the chickens and cleaned out the old hay from their coop, replacing it with fresh stuff. I checked all the plants in all the gardens and watered and trimmed and harvested when appropriate. I checked the water tanks. I kept the sprawling blackberries at bay with a machete. I split all the firewood and kept it stacked neatly inside next to the wood stove, which was our only source of heat. I quickly became proficient with an ax and maul, and as the weeks went by, I noticed myself developing strength.

I fell in love with the farm, with the country life— with its rhythms and with the changing seasons.

I spent many days down at the river swimming, canoeing, fishing, reading, and bathing. There were never other people around. We were the kings and queens of our world, and it was a good and simple life. I went to bed early each night, exhausted from the day's work, for the first time in my life.

When I first arrived, I stayed in a little RV down by the river, and there was a fat spider in the corner, but I didn't mind him. Sometimes, I woke to a chicken in the doorway, clucking curiously at me.

After a few weeks, the nights were growing colder, and the farmer let me stay in the attic in the farmhouse, for which I was very grateful.

Then, there she was. She was the farmer's eldest daughter.

We started doing chores together. She taught me so many things—how to gently handle the chickens, how to tell if an egg was bad, how to start a tractor, where to find mushrooms, how to swing an ax properly, how to siphon gas, and most importantly of all—how to cook.

I went to the ocean for the first time with her. We spent a lot of time together, and after a few months—well, we liked each other.

One late night, we stole out of the farmhouse, and we ran down to the river and jumped in, splashed around, and laughed in the dark with only the moon watching us. We fell in love, and we had to confess it.

At first, the farmer was taken aback, but he wasn't angry. He couldn't be. We were truly in love. We were best friends. We were so alike, despite coming together so randomly from thousands of miles apart.

She was an old soul, and unlike any other girl I'd met. I was twenty-two years old, and she was eighteen.

In my second year in Oregon, we got sheep. Twelve ewes—all pregnant. They fit in nicely on the farm, and the farmer taught me all about their needs and how to treat them. Soon enough, the ewes were having their lambs, and our flock quickly grew. Many of the ewes had twins, and we had adorable little lambs scampering and hopping around the fields.

Sometimes, sheep would escape from the pen—and being the younger man, I was tasked with retrieval, which meant slowly stalking them, creeping up as quietly as I could before tackling them to the ground and tying a rope to them so I could lead them back to the pen. I once tackled three sheep in one fell swoop, though they dragged me through a barbed wire fence before giving up.

One of the lambs was rejected by her mother, and without her nourishing milk, she would've died. I couldn't just watch the lamb in the field, left all by herself, so I scooped her up into my arms, and took her back to the farmhouse. The farmer taught me how to make a homemade version of the mother's milk, which contained the vital nutrient, colostrum, and I kept that tiny lamb in my room, and I bottle fed her. I named her Lucy.

Lucy would follow me all around the farm, always right behind me, prancing and hopping along with excitement. She would come to me when I called and suck eagerly on the bottle. When she got big enough to not need the bottle anymore, I found a local family who was looking for a sheep to be a companion to their sheep, and when they assured me that Lucy would be a pet—and not end up in the freezer—I handed her over to a smiling little boy and girl.

Time went by, and I lived the country life, learning new skills all the time. The daughter and I were happy together. We didn't have much need for other young people. There weren't very many to be found, anyway. Of course, I called my parents regularly and made sure they knew I was safe and happy, and well fed.

On my way out to Oregon, I hadn't been sure that it would work out. It might have gone horribly wrong in some way—but it didn't. Through it all, I remembered the life I had lived in Wisconsin, and I knew I had to keep going, even though it was a struggle, because I was striving, I was learning and growing, and I refused to look back.

Sometimes, I would look in the mirror, and I could hardly recognize the man I had become. In the country, I lived with the cycle of life—the cycle of life *and* death.

Of course, there were hard times out there, times the water lines would freeze in the winter, and times the water tanks ran dry when all you wanted to do was take a shower. Times when raccoons killed chickens, and times when crops would fail.

In the spring, we planted the gardens, in the fall, we harvested, and in the winter, we planted cover crops. I witnessed the birth of lambs, and kittens, and puppies, and horses, and the blooming of new flowers, and the growth of beautiful things.

I saw the death of things too. There was a cold January morning when a neighbor had to put down a horse that was gravely injured, and when the shot rang out, I knew it was the way it had to be. There was a dog that suddenly became very ill, and the medicine didn't help. She died in my arms, and I held her body and cried and didn't want to let her go. That was the lowest point I'd ever known. I had to remove the remains of the chickens that were killed by the raccoons, and I swore that I wouldn't let another one be taken.

In the summer, the river was an idyllic stream, flowing gently by, fit for swimming and wading and grabbing crawfish from the rocky bottom through the clear water. In the winter, with all the rain and mountain snow, the river became a raging torrent, and it came up into the fields. I learned to respect its might and its changing whims. At times, whole trees, with their root systems intact, would go floating by, having been torn from the ground somewhere upstream.

After some time had gone by, I knew that I needed to find a job where I could earn a paycheck. I needed to earn some money in addition to helping out with the chores.

There wasn't much around out there if you were trying to find work, unless you wanted to be a logger, which I did not. The biggest place around was Camp 18, a restaurant on Highway 26 between Portland and Seaside, which was about forty-five minutes from the farm in Mist. I applied for a job there, and heading into the summer season, I got hired on as a dishwasher.

So, there I was, in effect, with two jobs. One was at home—where I'd been for a year and a half—and I had no intention of moving off the farm. The other one was scrubbing dishes at a huge, very busy restaurant filled with waves of tourists. Compared to work on the farm, the dish pit seemed like nothing, and the cooks and waitresses must have thought I was crazy for the way I silently toiled away.

Once, a cook came up to me and said loudly, "Kyle! You've been back there nonstop for ten hours. Take a break, man."

I started taking breaks after that, but despite being the lowest rank in that busy restaurant, I enjoyed it, and I never called in sick, and I always showed up on time. I suppose that's what got the attention of the chef, because after a few months, he asked me if I wanted to be a cook. I knew it would be better than the dish washing position, and it would pay better too, so I agreed and started my training right away.

I cooked at Camp 18 for almost three years, learned a lot as a line cook, and progressed from working the deep fryer to being the opening breakfast cook. All the while, I was living on the farm, and the daughter and I were still happy, life was busy and beautiful, and I felt like I had found the meaning I was searching for. I worked hard, as hard as I could, and always felt fortunate and humbled for the life I had forged for myself.

After Camp 18, I cooked at the Elderberry Inn, and after that, in July of 2013, I took a few weeks off and hung out on the farm. I sat down by the river, and as I watched it flow idly by, I thought about my life—where I had been, and where I was.

It was during this time, after more than three years together, that the daughter and I began to grow apart. We scraped every ounce of love from our time together that we could, and we enjoyed it, but just as love is strong, it sometimes fades away and dies. It must be constantly nurtured, lest it shrivels up like any garden plant, longing to be bountiful but devoid of the care that it deserves.

While living in rural Clatsop County over the years, I came to discover Astoria. For one, it was the closest "big" city to our farm—we had relocated to another property in Jewell, sheep and all—and it was where I went to deposit my paychecks, and to buy groceries, for the most part.

I always thought it was a lovely town—sitting there at the mouth of the Columbia River—but being so in love with country life, and with the farmer's daughter and her family, I hadn't considered living there. Faced with the lack of jobs after working at two of the major employers to be found in Jewell, I began my hunt for jobs in Astoria.

The daughter was planning on going to school in Portland. I think she realized that our simple country life couldn't go on forever—which I had also realized. There comes a point when you have to consider whether being with someone is holding you back from self-actualizing, even if you love them very much.

After applying for a job at a dozen places and not hearing anything, late one night, I sent an email off to the least likely of places, to a place I thought I would never hear back from, and to a man I had only heard legends about—Uriah Hulsey at the Columbian Cafe. My email was short and to the point, and I was sure it would be doomed to some junk mail folder for eternity, when to my surprise, he called me on the phone and told me to come in for an interview.

I was hired, and that was that. I had a job in Astoria. It was late August. For the next six months, I commuted from the farm, and it was a forty-five minute drive over a long, winding, hilly, pothole-filled road. I started working nights, and I would leave in the early afternoon and get home late at night.

After a few weeks, I became the breakfast cook, and I had to leave early in the morning—as it was heading into winter—to get to the cafe on time. Many mornings, as I headed out for my long drive, it was pouring rain, and occasionally snowing. Sometimes, there were patches of ice, and other times, the winter storms were blowing with all their might.

I began to carry my chainsaw in my trunk, and on one occasion, a tree came down right in front of me. In the pouring rain, at 6:00 a.m., in the light of my headlights, I cut through that tree in order to get to work.

Many times, elk and deer would dart in front of me, sometimes leaping over the hood of my car. I narrowly missed them.

The months became increasingly difficult as I became more and more involved in my job and my commute became more hazardous. I would get home after working a long day and be in a bad mood. Unfortunately, I became just another grumpy boyfriend home from work, complaining about the drive.

I realized I couldn't live both lives. I had to move to Astoria. I had to be closer to my job. I was making new friends, and I was eager to hang out with them. I wanted to explore the city and its surroundings. Once again, somewhere new was calling, and this time it was a small city by the sea.

A few months before, I had gotten a puppy, a two-week-old chocolate lab and pit bull mix, who I named John Lennon. I finally found an apartment in Astoria that would let me have my dog and that I could afford. I signed all the paperwork and paid my deposit and first month's rent. February of that year, I became an Astorian.

It was also in February that the daughter and I broke up. Some things happened, due to the weakness of our relationship, which finally brought things to an end. I set about beginning the immense task of untangling our lives.

It took several trips out to the farm to gather my things, and it was all said and done. I said farewell to the farmer and thanked him for all the things he had taught me, for sharing his life with me, and for welcoming me into his family with open arms. We shook hands, and I drove my old pickup truck full of my belongings to my new apartment in Astoria.

I never saw the farmer again, nor did I go back to Jewell.

The transition from the wide-open spaces in the country, having acres to roam, to a one-bedroom apartment with a dog was not easy. It certainly was not something I had planned on when I brought John home with me.

Of course, we are not always at the helm of the great ship we call life, and we must deal with the changing winds.

My job at the cafe at least afforded me enough time to not have to think about everything that had transpired. In the quiet hours in the evenings at my apartment, I slowly began to process my journey and my experiences.

In the following months, I became truly independent for the first time since coming to Oregon—living alone and being responsible for my entire schedule. I enjoyed that time to the fullest and was a truly lucky guy to meet new people and make new friends. From one community to another, I only experienced welcoming people in Oregon who were eager to listen to my story and to tell me theirs.

In Astoria, I didn't have a garden. I had no chickens or sheep to check on. I turned on the faucet in the kitchen and the water came flowing out, but I didn't know where it came from. If it got cold in the winter, I could flip on an electric box, and my apartment got warm, and so, my ax and my chainsaw sat idly by.

I couldn't bring myself to throw my food scraps into the garbage after so many years spent composting and gardening. So, I'd gather them in a bucket with my coffee grounds and other things that would break down, and I'd take the bucket down into the long grass that grew between my apartment building and Young's Bay every so often. I'd dump it on the ground, hoping that at least, it would break down into soil, and that some worm would find it a suitable home.

I don't think the country will ever leave me. It's a part of me now. I know I must keep on striving. I can't look back—I have come so far.

Kyle McCarthy's next venture was at the Columbia Café in Astoria, where he continued working on his culinary skills.

"...we didn't know how to drive,
but that didn't bother us."

The Flat Tire
Blew Our Cover

Mary Montgomery

June and I were always doing things that we would have gotten in bad trouble for if our parents found out, so we were always very careful they never found out.

They did know we went up to the McCulloughs' every weekend to exercise the farm horses. But they didn't know we could imitate our mothers' signatures perfectly and often went up to the farm weekdays as well.

That was especially dangerous for me, as my older sister worked in the office at school, but not usually at the front desk. Except once, and then she kept a very straight face, which made me very happy. If she'd seen more than one faked excuse, I'm sure she wouldn't have been so obliging.

June and I always exercised the horses well. We rode them about four miles. The McCulloughs had raised horses for the Derby in the past and had a very long stable, about seventeen stalls. They had a huge tack room, its walls covered with every possible kind of tack: harnesses, saddles, bridles, brushes, etc., and all of the best quality.

The McCulloughs' son, Fred, taught us how to care for the horses, curry them down, put a blanket over them, and put them in their stalls. Fred had an intellectual disability—just a little bit.

The McCulloughs were very nice to us. They thought June and I were sweet, innocent young things. Sometimes, we would have cake and homemade ice cream with them. We had the run of the place, so one day we decided to explore beyond the stable. We found a big ol' barn with a wonderful old Model T Ford just sitting there.

When we were about to leave for the day, Fred came out to check on the horses. We said, practically in unison, "We'd sure like to have that old Model T out in the barn."

Fred said, "I'll let you have it for $5—if you promise you won't take any boys in it."

June and I immediately promised and said, "Okay, we'll pay you $5 for it, but we'll have to get up the money first."

It was the Depression, so getting $5 was not all that easy. But we were very ingenious and desperately wanted that Model T.

We decided to tell our folks we needed new summer shoes. My arches were high, so my feet were hard to fit, and mother always bought DeLessa Debs for me in the best shoe store in town. And they were expensive.

Kinney's Volume chain store had just come to town, and they had cheap shoes. June and I sneaked over there and got summer sandals that cost less than half what they would cost at any regular shoe store. Mine didn't quite fit, and I suffered all summer long—but quietly. The pain was worth it.

Between us, we had about $12 left over. We chipped in $2.50 apiece to buy the car. In the meantime, Fred had cleaned the car up, polished all the metal work, and put some gas in it—and it ran!

Of course, June and I didn't know how to drive, but that didn't bother us. We were way out in the country, and the road wasn't paved. But there wasn't a whole lot of paved road in those days, anyway. The T had one pedal that stopped it and one pedal that made it go forward. You did have to crank it—Fred showed us how—and we got pretty good at that.

You didn't have to have a license in those days. June and I drove it up and down the road until we considered ourselves very capable drivers. Gas only cost about fifteen cents a gallon, and we had lots of money left over from our shoe scam. We had enough for gas to last us quite a while.

Finally, summer vacation came, and we could go out to the farm on weekdays, legally. June and I decided to drive the Model T as far as Savoy, about seven miles away. That was a great adventure.

June knew an old man named Mr. Bushell near Savoy. We could turn off at the granary and go to Mr. Bushell's house. He'd give us apples to eat, and by that time, we'd always be pretty hungry. Mr. Bushell was best friends with my Uncle David Burrell. But Mr. Bushell didn't know of my relationship, and fortunately, we never met up with my uncle there.

One time, Mr. Bushell gave us eggs to take home to our parents. We thanked him very kindly and were careful not to break them on the way home, but we told our folks the eggs were from the McCulloughs. Luckily, our parents didn't know the McCulloughs.

One day when we were visiting Mr. Bushell, he said he wanted to show us something special. His house was very clean, but the only furniture we saw was a table and three chairs in the kitchen. The rest of the house was empty, but on the sun porch, there was a simple wooden coffin that he had constructed. It was well made, and Mr. Bushell was very proud of it.

He told us, "This is my last suit."

We were impressed.

It must have been late summer, because it was like going through a forest to get home. The corn was about ten feet high. The leaves almost met over the road.

We were such great drivers by then that we drove all over the twin cities where we lived—Urbana-Champagne, Illinois. We learned where all the gas stations were in both towns that were good, because we started to have flat tires. We didn't have enough money for new tires. Someone told us where we could buy used tires for fifty cents. New ones cost around $3.

Besides flat tires, we had to contend with patching our old tubes. We did get a little extra money babysitting, and we needed it all to keep our Model T on its wheels.

In the hot summer weather, it rained, and we would very quickly tilt the divided front windshields shut. Then, we would scramble to put up the isinglass side curtains. On the way back from Savoy one day in the rain, we saw a cyclone pick up a whole barn. Fortunately, it wasn't coming our way. We had a lot of fun those several months of spring and summer.

After school started again, when we were, as usual, changing a tire at a friendly neighborhood gas station, a fellow my folks knew passed by.

He asked, "Whose car is that?"

I immediately answered, "It's June's."

But later, he asked our friend, the service station man, who ratted on me. We were ordered to sell our Model T.

June and I never did take any boys in the car, not that we weren't attracted to boys, but we were also kind of scared of them. They made us nervous. We were only thirteen, not quite fourteen, a not so glamorous age.

We sold the Model T for the same amount we paid for it—$5. We even had a little trouble scratching up a customer, as it was 1931, the depth of the Great Depression. But, we finally found a buyer—Lil.

Lil's father was a doctor. Mine was too, but luckily, they didn't know each other, as they practiced in different cities. Lil was supposedly related to Russian royalty, and her mother thought nothing was too good for Lil. She allegedly started a chapter of the National Junior League, so Lil would be eligible to debut in Chicago.

The society editor of our twin city newspaper played up Lil and her mother's social climbing to great advantage. This didn't go over too well with most of the town, as that was when many people were out of work and even hungry.

Lil was also a gossip. She didn't like us, and she spread tales about us. June and I didn't like her either, and we may have spread our share of gossip concerning Lil.

June and I finally finished high school and started college. I had sense enough to major in art and music, both of which I liked and was good at. Poor June was stuck with a course much more difficult for her. Her father was a lawyer and insisted she take Logic—three times.

When she flunked it the third time, he gave her a year of hard labor working in a meatpacking factory in Chicago. I visited her once, and she didn't even have a window in her tiny little hotel room.

Eventually, June was reprieved. I don't remember if she ever passed Logic, but she finished in Education and taught school out West somewhere. She became friendly with a young man on the next ranch, and they married.

Unfortunately, we've lost track of one another, which is too bad. June surely was a lot of fun—especially when we had the Model T. That was a real joyride!

Mary Montgomery attended the University of Illinois, and then met and married a man who sang in the church choir with her. They had three children together.

Mary spent many later years painting portraits and scenes and playing the piano, and she was a concert-quality singer. She was a voracious reader, played Bunco, and enjoyed walks along the Astoria waterfront. Mary left this world in December 2016, a few months before her 100th birthday.

"Fight fire aggressively, having provided for safety first."

Thirtymile Fire Remembered

Norm Maxwell

In time for the 4th of July weekend 2003, I am dispatched to the Fawn Peak Fire Complex near Winthrop, Washington, as a helicopter crewman. The Fawn Peak and Sweet Grass fires were quickly contained at seventy and 150 acres, but the Farewell Fire is still roaring. It marches north into the wilderness between Winthrop and the Canadian border. Its eastern border abuts the old 2001 Thirtymile Fire's burn area.

Four other firefighters from Foster Helibase and I finish assembling a 15,000-gallon Heliwell portable water tank for heavy helicopters to dip up to 3,000 gallons of water at a time. We decide to pay our respects at the memorial for the four fire fighters who died on the Thirtymile. It is only ten miles up the Chewuch River Road between the confluences of the Chewuch and Andrews Creek, downstream, and Thirtymile Creek upstream.

A mile or so from where the pavement ends is a jumbled boulder field to the left of the road. An American flag juts from a metal socket nailed in a blackened fir snag. We park the van, and we get out.

A wall of mortared native stone stands at the end of a gentle asphalt ramp not far from the road. Embedded in the wall are four black marble panels with portraits of the dead firefighters etched in the smooth surface.

We gather and read the dates. Most of us were fighting fires before three of the people were born, and we continue to do so after their deaths.

Fire is a living organism. It comes into the world small and weak and can be stomped to death with a Vibram boot at birth. It eats and grows, grows and eats. It moves sometimes slowly, sometimes quickly.

It rests at night and is most active on hot afternoons. It creeps, stunted, through stony areas and waxes strong and fierce in thick brush and dead fuel. It reproduces, with firebrands cast skywards in hot updrafts to come down wherever—and live or die on their own—like jellyfish eggs.

Sometimes, it is a placid sheep, and you can walk up to it and take the food right out of its mouth. Other times, it is a roaring dragon and wants to kill with blind malice. I think that is what happened on July 10, 2001, in this pile of jumbled rock.

We look at the fine, flat sand bar in the Chewuch, not more than seventy meters from where the four died. The boulders might have looked like a good place to deploy shelters, perhaps, but there were a lot of fir needles and flammable leaf litter in the cracks, and the shelters would not seal effectively against the irregular surface. A whole twenty-person crew could have deployed its tinfoil fire shelters on the damp sand bar and survived. It was there two years ago.

We walk the short trails that thread through the rocks a little ways to where there are bronze plaques the size of saucers embedded in boulders where the four tried to live and failed.

Like at Storm King Mountain, firefighters leave things at this place, too. There is a fire shovel and a Pulaski with crew names written on the handles. A weathered teddy bear sits alone, and notes on write-in-the-rain paper are weighted down with rocks.

I read some of them and put them back.

Ubiquitous plastic water bottles are carefully placed on rocks along with metal Hot Shot crew emblems.

Firefighter caps and tee shirts abound with places and dates and fire names printed on them. A plastic floral arrangement with, "Love, Mom and Dad," written on it, has fallen over. And coins.

I see a worn Alcoholics Anonymous coin. That meant a lot to somebody.

There are heaps of coins on top of the gray stone crosses at Storm King. At first, I'd thought that the change was left by people who had not thought to bring some other memento to leave at the site, but now I think perhaps there is a more atavistic level to this.

Coins used to be placed over the eyes of the dead and in their mouths so they would have the toll to pay Charon for passage across the River Styx in the Underworld. It bears thinking about.

I take a laminated ten-by-eighteen card out of my pocket and slip it through a crack in the rocks. The card has the 10 Standard Firefighting Orders and 18 Watchout Situations listed on it.

No. 10: Fight fire aggressively, having
provided for safety first.

We all muse and reflect, and look at the trout in the neck-deep water of the Chewuch. A woodpecker hammers in the charred timber across the river. I pick up a white rock from the kill zone. I will put it next to the red one from Storm King on my front porch.

Nobody has much to say, and we drift back to the van to leave without a word being spoken.

Surveyors, woodsmen, and firefighters run in Norm Maxwell's family. He has surveyed for the Bureau of Land Management, and his duties included contract settling as a union representative, stump lording for tree planting, finding and hauling dead vehicles from Bureau of Land Management and Forest Service land, and fighting fires close-to-hand during fire season.

"...the sizzle of a lightning bolt
hit the ground..."

Becoming a Waterfinder

Mike Doney

When I was born in Portland, Oregon, my mother was in such a hurry to get back home to the farm, she left a handwritten note on my birth certificate saying, "Name will be sent later."

She decided to name me Orval Lee Doney, but my Uncle Charley called me Mike. He's the uncle who taught me you only have to wash the parts of plates you eat off of. I liked being Mike better than being Orval Lee.

"Don't cut the cord too short!" I heard just after my sister, Cleo, was born in our log house.

I was only three and too short to see up on the table. That remark was something to wonder about.

After Cleo arrived, our two-bedroom log house was just too small, so my family built a new house alongside it and used the cabin for a garage and shop.

Our place in Cave Junction, Oregon, had been the stagecoach stop between Grants Pass, Oregon, and Crescent City in northern California. The main road curved through the woods above our house and down the hill, and it passed directly through the big pole barn.

The barn had horse mangers and hay mows—rhymes with cows—a loft for storing hay and straw on both sides of the roadway, as well as cow stanchions to tie the cows to, also. My three older brothers often slept in these lofts. I had a private section above the cows where I liked to sleep.

There are many interesting noises in a barn at night.

48

Swallows who build mud houses under the roof ridges talk a lot in the dark. Cows chew their cud, and horses shift their weight around. And, sometimes, special noises like dawn roosters wake you up.

There were scary noises too. Once, in the dead of a dark, dark night, I was startled awake by a jolting, wrenching, loud, incredible crashing, crunching ear-splitting racket—then total silence. I was the only one in the barn, except for the animals. I had a kerosene lantern. I wondered if I should light it and take a look. I thought better of it and decided to lie low.

In the morning, I found out our big old hay wagon had been parked near the top of the hill. A cow or horse most likely found it good to rub on. The wagon broke loose and came down the road guided by an unseen hand, right into the barn. It had crashed into the barn boards directly below my loft bed.

I also have some good memories about a pretty little blue-eyed blonde named Norma Embree. She was probably my first love. She had good energy, and I liked her a lot.

We were together once at dusk when a meteor went over our heads. We heard it sizzling, and then we saw it. Hot red in the middle, dripping chunks off the tail end— a neat foam-like white material was around its body and its tail. It went over the hills, and later, we heard it had landed in the ocean, making a sound like thunder.

When she and her mother went back to California, I asked Norma to be sure and write—as soon as she knew how. We were five then. I never heard from her—my first major heartfelt loss.

I did learn to write—at Rockydale Grade School, a one-room school a mile away from home. It had eight rows of desks from smallest to largest, facing the teacher. A wood stove was on one side and a row of windows on the other. The water bucket was filled from the well with a big, long-handled pump. Two outhouses stood in back of the school.

My first teacher was an alcoholic. He would give the

assignments then put his feet up on his desk and go to sleep. The kids would go out to play. He was eventually caught drunk by a school board member. His bottle was in his desk. That ended his tenure.

I spent a lot of time hunting with my dad and brothers when I was young. I was responsible for bringing down both a three- and a four-point buck before reaching the eighth grade. I also managed to shoot myself in the wrist and the foot, with one shot, while climbing a pine tree to better stalk a deer.

When I reached home, I was hauled off to a doctor. He told me the river wasn't a good place to wash a wound. My ear stopped ringing eventually. It was a good lesson.

I graduated from Kerby Union High School in Kerby, Oregon, in 1942. Pearl Harbor had been bombed the December before. I decided to join the Navy. I had to send for my birth certificate, and a letter came back requesting a name. I had always been Mike, so I decided to be Mike on the certificate: Mike Orval Doney. Mother asked why I hadn't made it Michael—because I was Mike.

The Navy rejected me. My blood pressure was too high. I tried to get into the Merchant Marines. Rejected! The draft rejected me too.

The Siskiyou National Forest ranger told my dad a man had left a lookout job at Hayward Peak because it was too lonely. He asked if he knew of anyone who would go there as the replacement. A month's worth of food had already been packed in the nineteen miles by mules. It was a beautiful place. I spent two summers there watching for fires and enemy aircraft.

The telescope-like Osborne Firefinder was on a big rock on the peak. My tent was on a rock bench 600 feet below. The spring was another 600 feet below that. The Chetco River canyon was off to the south and west, and the Illinois River canyon was on the north and east. No one ever came except the mule packer, who brought supplies once a month.

Thunderstorms up there were interesting. I had been told to watch for them coming in and count the time between the lightning and the clap of thunder. This way, I would know when to unhook the wire from my two-way radio. The problem was, the mountain was sometimes the originating point of a storm.

The first time I found that out, dark, heavy clouds formed overhead. Initially, there was no lightning. But then, the sizzle of a lightning bolt hit the ground, and a tree right behind my tent took the shock. The clap of thunder was simultaneous. I was at ground zero!

I hurried into the tent where my radio was and reached down to unhook the antenna. Another loud crack like a gunshot—it was as if someone had hit me hard with a baseball bat. The jolt knocked me down.

I grabbed two sticks and unhooked the antenna then headed down off the peak at a high lope. I feared I might be targeted for the next lightning strike. My hair was long, and I could feel static electricity jumping around in it. It was scary.

In a case like this, I had been told to go down over the hill, hide in some low brush, and stay there. I did! Bolt after bolt of lightning came down all around me. I stayed low until the storm passed.

The next phase of my life began when I followed the pleasant voice of the girl on the adjacent forest lookout—sight unseen—to Corvallis, Oregon, to enroll at Oregon State College in forestry. Facing advanced algebra, I dropped out of college and began drifting around as young men do.

I tried logging and bought a Model A. I started for Chile with my buddy, Bert, who said the girls there were beautiful. But Bert liked to party, and we were broke before we got to the coast.

Then, it was working cattle and building fences. The Model A was transportation between jobs. When the bearings went out, I caught a ride with friends but on a curious whim gave my seat to a lookalike. The car hit a cement abutment, and my doppelganger was killed. That's when I first began to suspect I had a guardian angel.

The Gem Fruit Packing Plant was next. The season over, I peddled fruit and vegetables house-to-house with a friend, Collins. He introduced me to a pretty redhead from the big city of Seattle, Washington, who was visiting her aunt and uncle in Kerby, a small Josephine County, Oregon town near the California border.

I took Bety bullfrog hunting and noticed she had freckles and nice legs. I rescued her from a deep, cold pool when she got washed over the falls. She noticed me favorably.

After marrying in Seattle in 1949 and honeymooning down the coast, Bety and I rented a cabin in Kerby at Frederick's Motel. Our good friends began a shivaree with a blast of dynamite in the gulch behind the cabin. It rocked the windows and houses all around. Horns were honking, guns were fired off, and people were beating tin pans. People came crowding in and were very liberal with their bottles of booze.

A country custom is for an unmarried older brother to dance in a pig trough—so a pig trough was hauled in, and my unmarried older brother, Ralph, got to dance in it. The goings-on lasted well into the early morning. Several cars were parked in front of our cabin for a couple days before their owners recovered well enough to come for them.

I was back working in the woods, and Bety was pregnant when I caught my foot between two logs. When the doctor checked that out, he also noticed my ruptured appendix that had been giving me stomach cramps along with a 103-degree fever off and on for a year.

During a long recovery, our landlord, Jack McCracken, dropped by to pass the time of day. Out of the blue, he asked, "What do you know about dowsing?"

I replied, "Isn't that where you witch for water?"

Jack nodded and continued talking. "But there's a lot

more. There are systems in what looks like empty space—systems that have form and patterns. Dowsing, or water witching, is the recognition and feedback from certain of these systems."

My first thought was that this guy was some kind of nuts, but I was interested and listened as Jack went on.

"Almost anyone can learn to find systems of energy that have defined form and are invisible to most. All you need are the basic techniques that the waterfinder uses. You can tune in and recognize different energies just by asking to find them individually. It's as if the thought plays a part in recognizing the different patterns and can differentiate between underground water, a gas line, a septic line, or other energy patterns."

I still thought he was off his rocker, but Jack taught me to use a bent wire, a forked stick, and eventually a map or just my mind, to find most anything: a deer, fish, grouse, and water, gas, and sewer lines. I learned to locate minerals and even malevolent energy, how to block it, and how to protect the body from it.

From starting out as a lookout, to being a logger, and all the jobs in between, I never expected to become a waterfinder. But Jack had me hooked, and I've enjoyed the art of dowsing ever since.

Mike Doney was born in Portland, Oregon, and was raised on the family ranch in Cave Junction, Oregon. In 1949, he met and married the love of his life, Bety Jean Pearl. They were married for fifty-six years.

Mike was introduced to dowsing in 1951. He spent the rest of his life studying and teaching the art. Mike taught water dowsing at Portland Community College and Clackamas Community College and founded the Northwest Society of Dowsers. He retired from the Oregon Liquor Control Commission in Portland in 1982. He enjoyed his dogs, garden, golf, hunting, fishing, camping, friends, and life.

"...cars weren't manufactured
with seatbelts back then."

Point of Contact

Bruce Berney

"I just got the call about your wreck," the
Washington State Patrol trooper said as he looked my
car over.

His quick arrival surprised me because my car had
hardly come to rest, and I was just beginning to assess
the damage to its right side.

"Huh, it's not as bad as I was told. You sure are lucky
the post kept you from going over the bank. Looks like
your car's okay."

Having attended the October 1959 Homecoming
Weekend at University of Puget Sound in Tacoma,
Washington, I'd been driving east over Snoqualmie Pass
on U.S. Highway 10 (now called I-90) when the accident
happened.

Actually, you can't call it an accident because I was
going sixty miles per hour on purpose. I was eager to get
home. I had rented a room in the house of an elderly
lady in Soap Lake, Washington, where I was the new
high school English teacher at twenty-four years old.
This was my first job out of the Army. With six
preparations each day, I knew I'd be up late getting
ready for Monday classes.

One should never be complacent when driving on
mountain roads. Here, a couple miles east of the summit,
the highway was four lanes wide but had just a guardrail
separating the inside lanes. From time to time in winter,
the steep slopes on the north side of the highway spewed

life-threatening avalanches.

Looking south, the forested land dropped away into alpine mists. It was the first Sunday afternoon of hunting season, and snow had just begun to fall, so the highway had not yet been sanded.

Homecoming wasn't all that great. Expecting to meet many of my buddies at the formal dance at the Field House, I had written to Elizabeth, a girl who had been a freshman when I was a senior. I didn't know her well but felt lucky to have a date lined up.

To my chagrin, just before the dance, I learned she was a homecoming princess. Although she didn't wear the jeweled crown, I was out of my element with all the attention she was getting. By then, I'd realized I was a stranger on campus, and none of my old friends attended the dance. Worse yet, I'd never danced well, a fact of which Elizabeth was unaware when she'd accepted my invitation.

It felt good, once the dance ended, to be speeding back to central Washington in my blue-gray 1956 Volkswagen Beetle. I had bought it from a dealer in D.C. where I had been stationed and driven it across the country. I had always heard Beetles handled well in snow, so I was having a fun time passing all the big American cars.

How surprised I was when I realized my car was spinning once or twice, ending on the right shoulder beside a lone concrete post, which kept the car from rolling down a forty-foot bank. I shudder when I remember cars weren't manufactured with seatbelts back then.

The trooper had said my car looked fine, and I may as well continue my journey. By then, he'd gotten another call and realized the big wreck was a mile down the road. I'd passed it on my way, but it didn't give me any satisfaction, for I now had troubles of my own.

I soon realized there were several things the trooper hadn't noticed. The first was that the clutch cable had broken. That had happened a few months before, but I'd had it repaired.

At that time, I'd learned that by rolling forward in second gear, the car could start by compression. I couldn't shift up to third or fourth gear, though, so traveling slowly then was a given. That didn't bother me, for by that time, traffic was traveling bumper-to-bumper at twenty miles per hour in the right hand lane.

The next thing I noticed, and it was pretty obvious, was that whenever I moved the steering wheel even slightly, the horn would blow. So, all the way to Ellensburg—about forty miles—I was nervously tailgating the car in front of me with my single-tone horn blaring beep, "Be-beep, beep!"

Perhaps I should have pulled off the road and disconnected the wires, but I knew if I did that:

> (a) I might get stuck in the snow since I couldn't use first or my reverse gear.
>
> (b) It would be hard for me to get back into the solid line of traffic since my motor had to start by compression and couldn't idle.
>
> (c) My foot brake didn't work.

I vowed that when I got to Ellensburg, I'd coast into the first gas station, hope the hand brake would work, ask for free overnight parking, and hitchhike to Soap Lake.

My luck held firm. At the service station, I begged a ride from a man going to Moses Lake. I had him let me off at the lonely junction near the town of George, Washington, where Highway 283 provided a twenty-mile shortcut to Ephrata.

When I'd left home, I certainly hadn't expected the blizzard. At Ellensburg, I was cold in my light clothing, so I took the fake Navajo blanket I kept on the back seat with me.

At the George junction, I draped the blanket over my head and clutched it tightly under my chin while holding my small suitcase in my other hand.

I'm sure I looked quite pitiful. The first person to

come along stopped. On his way to Coulee City, he gave me a ride to my house at Soap Lake.

On Monday, I phoned a body shop, which had a mechanic who could fix my then unusual foreign car. In a few weeks, I took the bus to Ellensburg and joyfully drove my precious car home. It refrained from honking all the way.

Several months later, while returning from visiting my brother in Bellevue, Washington, driving east again over Snoqualmie Pass, I recognized the concrete post by the chasm—now devoid of snow.

Stopping, I saw a smudge of my car's blue-gray paint. I said a silent prayer of gratitude for the highway crew that had put the post on the very spot where I had needed it that snowy October Sunday.

Bruce Berney was born in 1935 in Walla Walla, Washington. He attended the University of Puget Sound in Tacoma. Just out of college, he was drafted and served as a first aid man in an Army camp. In 1966, the City of Astoria mounted a nationwide search for a new public library director. Bruce was selected and held the position for thirty years. Since retiring, Bruce has been writing light verse. In 2005, he self-published his first and only book, Lewis and Clark's Digital Clock.

"We were ready to die rather than live under Communist rule."

Escape from Communist Hungary

Zola Zoltan Bokor

I'd been planning to escape since I was nine years old because basically, as a kid, I saw Communism as a big lie. The Communist Party emphasized how great the Russians were—they gave us all freedom. But we knew it wasn't freedom we had. We had been free, but they took it away.

My father was a goldsmith. He had a good business. He had a store and made beautiful art. People trusted my father to make their gold into rings and other lovely things. My father worked hard until he died when he was seventy-two. He stepped off a streetcar and was hit by a motorcycle.

Father's name was Stephen. Mother's name was Phluska. He called her Ilone, and a lot of pet names: my little goldfish, my small bird. My mother too worked hard. Their first two sons died as infants during wartime—different stories were told as to how—conditions were so bad.

The first thing the Communist government did was shut down all enterprise. They allowed no private business—they even took away sewing machines. But, our neighbors needed rings—wedding rings, made from pieces of gold.

My father continued to work. He had a table with a box and compartments for his tools on top, and he put a cloth over that. When he made gold rings, he would go out into the woods, as far away as he could, to fire and melt the gold and to hammer it into shape. He could not make the noise near the house.

There was a certain code about how much gold you could own. The government restricted you. If they found out you had extra, they ripped you off—they stole it. Communism was especially strict in the 1950s under Khrushchev.

One day, someone told on my father—turned him in. The police took my father away. They beat and tortured him for 100 days, not counting the jail sentence—two years. They wanted to know where he hid the gold, silver, and precious stones. What he had in his shop, they took, but they were looking for more.

They took my mother away because she wouldn't tell on her husband and sentenced her to hard labor. Fortunately, her labor was sewing, a better fate than just sitting in a cell. It made the time go by faster.

My father went to jail three times in the fifties. Every time after my father came home from jail, he began working again. When he was out, he did his work, and we lived well. But when he was in jail, we didn't live too well. We lived with our mother's mother. Our grandma kept us alive, and we never went hungry.

My brothers and I lived with her on the outskirts of Budapest, Hungary. We had a garden and a pig once a year—all the meat and all the fat. Sometimes, we only had bread, but we never starved. Grandma's bread was good—very crusty and very heavy. I'm talking about real bread—not like ordinary American bread you squeeze like a sponge.

She had a wood stove. She would use the oven to toast a big slice of bread on a fork—toast one side, then the other. Grandma put garlic and then bacon grease on it. We had lots of tea and very nice toast. Very good, very tasty.

Life was not as good as here in America, though, where welfare feeds people without food. In Hungary, there was only your family to help.

Mother's family had connections. They were in the restaurant business. When I was fourteen and finished eighth grade, she put me in the best cooking school in Budapest—a fancy place that had all the fancy stuff. I worked as a cook for four days and then spent two days at school.

We cooked for kings: Haile Selasse, Abdul al Salal, the German Embassy, the king of Yemen, and Khrushchev—he was the same as a king—and a lot of other Communist leaders. Khrushchev came to the school with many cooks and brought his own smoked sturgeon.

The other students and I cooked when we did a banquet for eight hundred in Parliament. Fifty waiters took in wine for a toast. I learned how the people at the top level of the government ate—French cooking for the kings. After the meal, a speech was given in the cupola—the rotunda.

The Communists said everybody was equal, but when we served their banquets, they ate big fancy roasts with aspic. We decorated every plate, like a piece of art. At least a dozen or more chefs and I worked for two days. We prepared breast of pheasant, but the breast meat is dry, so we threaded bacon through them all and then roasted them for an hour.

The banquet was in a large room—a 100- or 200-foot room. The food was on big silver platters on one side of the table. Fifty waiters stood on the other side to serve. There was much hot food: ham, sliced goose liver, and big, round links of sausage. There was also cold food—everything you can imagine: roast beef, salami, stuffed chicken, veal cutlets, liver pâté, and a big spread of vegetables.

The basic salad was called a French salad: potato, green peas, pickles, and carrots mixed with mayonnaise—everything cut in small squares. Very colorful. This was used as the base in the middle of the large plate, under the meat. It was garnished with whole parsley, flowers from radishes, and carved mushrooms—three-dimensional truffles.

Some meat was made into sculptures brushed with liquid aspic and jellied aspic served in squares. There was also a tall fruit basket filled with grapes, bananas, and other fresh fruits. And, there was dessert! Everything was beautiful.

The cooking school also had a bakery side. It was a big place, and all the bakers did a beautiful job making fancy, fancy cakes, and strudel too.

Khrushchev just walked past the banquet table and waved. He was always afraid of being poisoned. He ate in another room, and his secretary took his food to him. First, samples of all the food was put into jars and taken into another room where scientists tested everything. There was never a chance to poison him.

I went into the Army when I was eighteen—mandatory—and came out when I was twenty.

One day while drinking a couple of beers with my brother, George, I told him I was planning to escape.

He said, "Me too."

We had never told anyone before. We never told anyone else, except our older brother, Stephen, because if the Communists heard, they would say you were betraying the country.

But our father was wise. He laughed and said, "We don't mind you boys leaving—just don't come back," pretending to tease us. He knew we were planning something.

In the Army, I took up flying. I flew small planes and gliders. They're the best. No engines. But my brother and I decided to just go on foot. We had a compass and a map. It was summertime 1970.

We wanted to go to Yugoslavia. It was also Communist, so they agreed to give us a passport—but it still took months and months. Then, like a miracle, one day, we got the passports—a visa—to go to Yugoslavia. That was our plan. Next, we would escape to Italy. George was eighteen. I was twenty-one.

We went to Yugoslavia. It took us two weeks to get close to the Italian border. We had to be extra careful. First, we went to Puhla, a little town near there. The last night we spent in Yugoslavia, we stayed at a woman's house. No, she was not someone we knew—her house was just close to the border.

George and I left all our luggage at the house and just took a backpack and our map and compass. We went to a restaurant, ate a piece of smoked fish—just a snack, not a real meal—and had a beer. Even going in there was risky. We were in a hurry and looking out for danger.

When a border guard came in, we left quite quickly. We went to the woods and out into the forest. From there, we walked through the forest, about ten miles to the Italian border.

When we got to a point, high up, we looked down and saw a long row of cars. I realized it was the checkpoint for the border—with the feeling like my heart was beating right in my throat. George and I kept in the woods and the mountains, checking the map to be sure we were walking the right direction.

We'd been waiting so many years—we were so close to freedom. The excitement built up. We'd never done anything like this before. We were ready to die rather than live under Communist rule. It was a one of a kind feeling.

The mountain was rocky there. We would stand on one rock and run to the next rock, or maybe a bush. It was getting darker. That was good. We would be under cover. It was interesting that sometimes when we needed light, the moon came out. We could see to run to the next spot.

We saw two border guards—their silhouettes. We could see them very clearly. We had to do something, hide somewhere. There was grass so tall—as high as our knees—so we just lay down in the grass. The guards were coming right at us.

George had a piece of grass stuck in his throat. He

started to cough just as the guards were passing by. I grabbed George, almost choking him, and thank God, we didn't make too much noise.

After that, there were still a couple obstacles to go through such as the barbed wire along the border. Thankfully, it was quite low and wasn't too well kept. We were able to climb over it.

Some countries had less guarded borders than others. The Yugoslavian border was not as tall or as wide as the Berlin Wall. At another place along the Yugoslavian border, there were stainless steel plates, which would chime like bells, so we lay down and rolled over them.

It was pitch dark when we came to a valley filled with roses. We felt their petals but didn't smell them. We were too excited.

Our older brother, Stephen, worked for the Army fixing tanks, and he had made a big knife—as a gift for us—from a tank tread. We used it to cut at the bushes, but halfway through the valley, we lost the knife!

By the time we got through the rest of the rose bushes, our clothes were ripped in many places, and our skin was bleeding. It was about midnight. We were up high in the mountains. We would not know where we were until the morning.

My brother said, "No, no. Let us go on. We cannot stay here. We don't know where we are. We don't know if we are safe."

It was not like crossing the street. You needed to make sure you had passed into the other country.

Finally, while it was still dark, but almost morning, we found a road and saw a sign. The sign was in Italian. We recognized it right away. The sign said "Padliciano." We hugged each other. We cried. The joy we felt was incredible!

Soon, we found watermelon growing on the side of the road. We were so thirsty, we each ate a whole one. After that, we just walked on down the road.

That early summer morning, we saw a man coming

toward us with a dog—a German shepherd. We thought he was some kind of government man, maybe from the border patrol, but he was just a man from the country—an old timer. He knew immediately we were refugees.

The man said, "Come with me. My house is just down the road."

He took us in. He fed us breakfast. Even though he did praise Mussolini, he never liked Hitler. He was a good man. He was very happy for us to be free.

It took us a while to get out of Italy and to the United States. We were even in jail a few days. Finally, a man signed for our release in immigration. He had a business in New York City—he needed cooks for his restaurant. Not only was he pleased with us, but he was also retired from cooking at his German-Hungarian restaurant, and I became the head chef. My brother was the evening chef.

Unfortunately, the situation became bad. Our boss got involved with the Mafia. He was going to the racetrack every day, and he lost a lot of money. The Mafia came to the restaurant because of the cooking. Even though it was German-Hungarian, when the Mafia guys came in, I would make anything they wanted—even Italian.

After two years there, the restaurant had to close down because the boss didn't pay the taxes. The IRS came and said, "You have one half hour to leave."

We left the food on the steam table and walked out. The boss borrowed money from the Mafia to pay the taxes, and we opened again. Then, the Mafia warned the boss many times to pay, but he kept gambling, playing horses at the racetrack—all kinds of games, like the Daily Double. He was hooked on it.

The Mafia beat him up many times. He had an eighteen-year-old son, a big football player. Finally, the Mafia killed the boy. They hung him on the West side—the dark side of America.

We stayed a couple more years, and then we left. Our next job was in the Rockefeller building on the sixty-ninth floor—the Rainbow Room. I cooked for

Duke Ellington. He came into the kitchen, and I said I would cook anything he wanted. He liked the Oysters Rockefeller.

It was not long before the Mafia took that place over, too. When I started there, it was a French restaurant. The Mafia bought it, and it became an Italian one.

In about a year, I left. I cooked next in the Exxon Building, on the thirty-fifth floor, for Morgan Stanley—for Mr. Morgan and a lot of big shots.

After cooking here and there for a few more years, my last cooking job was in the New Yorker Hotel, owned by the Reverend Sun Myung Moon. It's a beautiful building, right next to Madison Square Garden. He owned other buildings too, and we became friends.

In 1972, when George and I were still working in New York City, we bought tickets for our folks to visit. They were here in the US for about a month. We went a lot of places, like Niagara Falls. We had a good time. They liked it here, but they didn't want to stay. They wanted to die at home.

My brother, Stephen—two years older—is also still in our homeland. He is in a good business—the wine business. He started under Communism, which was a miracle in itself. His wife, also from Hungary, is in the tour business. Together they make good money. They have one son.

My brother, George, stayed in New York City—never moved after we came to America. He cooked for thirty years at different places and was a wonderful cook. He went to same school I did. But, he got tired of cooking, so he began driving a taxi. He loved to drive and made good money.

Finally, I saw him again after nineteen years. He married a teacher from Hungary, and they had two sons. I married Sandy Delano—related to FDR—and we had five kids: Konlim, Jinju, Stephen, Christopher, and Zoli.

After leaving the New Yorker Hotel, I next spent fifteen years fishing. I fished all over the East Coast, the Banks, and Key West. Then, I sailed on a ship from

Alabama around through the Panama Canal to Alaska. That was a trip! The ship almost went down.

Finally, I fished for two years in Astoria, Oregon—dragging. Then, the fishing got slow because of new regulations.

My neighbor was doing a wood business, and he taught me. He had cancer, and he was still working, but he was getting in bad shape—his back. He wanted to sell.

It came at the right time. I was running out of unemployment checks. I bought his business, his tools, and his wood. He built gazebos, but I expanded into building all kinds of stuff—birdhouses, woodcarvings, everything I could do.

The business did well. Thank God for the tourists—and everything else.

Zola Zoltan Bokor is descended from kings. His family is named for them. However, he chose his first name, Zola, for himself when he came to this country—after the brilliant French novelist.

Zola says, "America is good because of the freedom. The four freedoms are important so that you won't hear a knock at the door in the middle of the night."

Zola has never looked back, and he is glad that his children receive the freedom he and George faced such danger to escape for.

After his culinary experience in New York City, and between fishing expeditions on the East Coast, Zola took art courses in Florida. He is a fine artist with pen or pencil as well as a wood sculptor.

"I squirmed and wriggled myself
back out of the hole."

A Bundle of Bones

Brian F. Harrison

What woke me this morning was a cockroach's
antennae tickling the fine hairs in my ear. Three others
crawled across my face—fewer than yesterday, so I think
things are looking up in my relationships with the
animal kingdom.

I can't complain. Since I was flown here for free to
help with the documentary, I'm perfectly willing to put
up with a few insects.

At this morning's production meeting, Giuseppe, the
Chief Scientist, said Andrea and I would be examining
human bones on film. He also wanted footage of us
gathering more remains from a basalt cavern near the
enormous stone heads at our archaeological site of Ahu
Runga.

Then our part would be done—two physical
anthropologists commenting on the differences between
these skeletons and those of Polynesia and Peru. Where
did these people come from—East or West? If we could
answer that, we'd be moderately famous. If not, we'd
have had a free trip to Easter Island in the South Pacific.

Director Thierry wanted a table full of bones for the
filming. Yesterday, Giuseppe indeed found several more
burials in rocks and caves near the site, but they were
nineteenth century, and some were in boxes. While
Thierry had no compunctions about grabbing whatever
he could find, wherever, for his filming, Giuseppe
refused to disturb the recent Catholic graves. I think it's

the difference between "ancestor" and "grandfather" for him and possibly a strong Catholic upbringing.

The morning was entirely taken up with filming in the yard next to our house beneath the avocado and lime trees. We had some weathered, fragmented human bones from some archaeological site, and Thierry brought out a bag of old sheep bones he had found somewhere. (I didn't want to ask.)

When it came time to film, the sheep bones were placed on the table along with the human bones, reference books, calipers, and magnifiers. Andrea and I measured, peered, recorded, and generally studied the bones for the film. We each taped a series of spiels, his in Italian and mine in English, about bones and those who used to be wrapped around them.

We touched on genetics, on the population variability of the ancient Easter Islanders, on their general health and the effects of cannibalism. Finally, we discussed evidence for their origins, East or West, in a mélange of English and Spanish with Andrea carrying most of the scientific and linguistic load.

We spent several hours after lunch cleaning the site of Ahu Runga, pulling up grass to get an idea of the distribution of hearths, gardens, cairns, and windbreaks, and to expose a platform with its stone heads toppled in tribal warfare. The platform itself (locally called an ahu) is composed of slabs of petroglyph-carved volcanic tuff—rock made of volcanic ash—overlooking a grove of palms and the white sands of Anakena Beach. There are caverns within the lava field, and Giuseppe asked me to search one beneath the ahu on camera.

As bones were discovered, I tried to identify them: sheep, rat, horse, and dog. When my eyes adjusted to the dim inside of the cave, I saw a bundle of human bones on a rock shelf against the wall. Long bones tied up with a rotten cord. I had only to reach in and collect them for analysis, then replace them.

But as I stretched across the darkness, I found they were just beyond my fingertips, so I squirmed farther into the narrow passage until I could just reach them with one last push. My fingers touched the remains of arms and legs. No pelvis, ribs, or skull, but definitely human. I replaced them on their ledge and tried to wriggle back out of the cave.

I discovered I was stuck like a cork, plugging the gap between the basalt boulders. I couldn't crawl forward or backward, and it was then that I began noticing rats scurrying among the rocks surrounding me—big European rats twitching their whiskers, observing me with their beady eyes.

Taking deep breaths to stay calm, and wishing I were skinnier, I put one hand on the rock below me and the other against the flat stone on the roof of the grotto. I squirmed and wriggled myself out of the hole like being born feet first into the hot sun.

I had noticed patterns of holes in the flat rock as I pushed against it, so as soon as I was free, I clamped a pencil flashlight between my teeth and slid back into the cave, this time face-up. When I got my eyes to focus that close, I found I was staring at a petroglyph of Make-Make, creator god of Rapa Nui, with his comically large eyes and long nose, and at a row of dots and straight lines carved into the basalt, which I saw was an ancient altar stone. My neck grated as I twisted my head to follow the pattern.

This maneuver freed my hips and shoulders, and I again inched feet-first out of the tunnel, scraping myself on the rough volcanic rock, leaving a trail of bloodstains to mark my passage. The cameraman and sound technician got it all on tape and thought the images would have looked more dramatic if the rats had attacked me.

Today was unusually hot, and tonight, the skin of my arms is still bubbling with blisters, looking like something from a bucket of deep-fried chicken. I should not be thinking that way on an island with a documented history of cannibalism.

Tonight, after rinsing off the island's dust, I noticed an overturned cockroach, like the one in my ear this morning, become immediately surrounded and consumed by hundreds of small ants. Before I crawl into bed, I believe I'll put in my earplugs.

Brian F. Harrison was born in 1947 in Spokane, Washington. He earned a Master of Arts in Sociology in 1971 from Gonzaga University and taught anthropology and sociology at Clatsop Community College in Astoria, Oregon. During the summers, Brian worked as an archeologist, excavating at sites in Oregon, Washington, Alaska, Wales, Peru, and Easter Island. He retired in 2002.

An avid writer, Brian authored two books of poetry, Landscapes of Memory *and* Winter Companions, *a novel,* Chasing Shadows, *and numerous magazine and journal articles on archaeology and science. He also appeared in two archaeology documentaries on the Discovery Channel. In 2015, Brian passed away.*

"...if you didn't learn quickly,
you didn't last long."

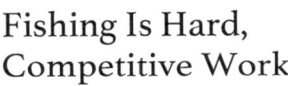

Fishing Is Hard, Competitive Work

Ralph Peitsch

One day, a fellow asked me, "Just how hard is commercial fishing?"

"You're a dairy farmer, aren't you?"

"Yes."

"Well, pretend this bay out here is one big field full of cows, and many farmers are all out there. Each farmer has twelve hours to go out, round up, and milk all the cows he can."

"That does sound pretty hard."

"But that's not all. First, you have to go out and find where the cows are. And then, there are poacher farmers out there milking your cows as fast as you round them up."

That's an idea of how hard and competitive commercial fishing is.

The term gillnet fishing has been around since Peter and Paul fished in the Sea of Galilee. They fished all night then, the same practice that we use today. We fish at night so the fish won't see the net.

Gillnetting is much different from seine netting. Seine nets have a mesh too small for the target fish to get its head through. So, the net essentially surrounds or corrals the fish.

Gillnets are designed to be invisible in the water. When the target fish unknowingly swims into the net, its gills become entangled in the mesh, trapping it.

When loaded with fish, the net is pulled in by winding it around a large, hydraulically operated drum—like a huge fishing reel. As the nets come onto the boat's stern, the men—working quickly and using picking hooks—pick the fish out of the net one at a time and load them into brailers, which line the fish lockers. It's a lot of hard work.

In older days of sailboat fishing in Bristol Bay, Alaska, boats were thirty feet long with a two-man crew: a skipper and a boat puller. The boat puller was called that because he would row the boat. He would be pulling on the oars while the skipper picked the fish out of the net.

When the boat was moving, it took both of them to work the sails. The term boat puller is still used today, though now he picks the net and the skipper runs the boat.

When fishing was no longer allowed on the Columbia River during June and July, it was easy for the Columbia gillnetters to move up north because everything was supplied: boats, nets, board, room, even extra blankets for the boat, and all else except your clothes. They changed over from sailing ships in 1952 so all the boats had engines.

If you were a big, strong guy, and could work twenty hours a day, even if you didn't know much at first, they'd hire you on. But if you didn't learn quickly, you didn't last long.

When we worked up there in 1967, our company, Peter Pan Seafoods, paid for our plane tickets and all supplies, including three nets. We had to sew the three net shackles together—150 fathoms total made a net.

I never heard of anyone ruining a net, as there was nothing in the way but salmon. Occasionally, though, a big beluga would hit the net and make a hole in it that you would have to mend.

The Alaska Department of Fish and Game set the fishing regulations. Twelve hours was a regular fishing period—then they'd close the time and maybe give you twelve hours the next day.

The cannery that provided all the equipment took thirty percent of the proceeds from the catch. We got seventy percent. That was our wages. Most skippers split it evenly with their pullers.

In 1968, the third of July, on the west side of Bristol Bay, we laid out the net, and it sunk with the weight of fish—over 3,000 in one haul! Nine ton—18,000 pounds. We hauled in two nets in one half hour. We filled the cargo net bags in each of the fish lockers. Then, we filled the cabin, the bunks, and every other possible place.

One shackle of net was still out there. We couldn't haul in the fish from it, or we would sink the boat. If we'd just left it out there, even marked with a buoy, someone else might have hauled it in. So we kept the motor running slow and hauled the third shackle of gear behind us to the cannery.

It took us about twelve hours from the time we started to the time we delivered. The 3,000 fish were worth about seventy cents apiece. That came out to about $2,100. We split it two ways, so one-half was $1,050. Divided by twelve hours, each partner made $87.50 per hour. Not bad for 1967.

In the early 1980s, about 3,000 Oregon gillnetters and/or trollers caught salmon. In 2002, only 467 Oregon boats were out there. Washington State was down to seventy-five from 2,000 boats.

The 2001 Oregon fleet landed about the same volume of Coho and Chinook as in 1985, but it earned less than half as much in real dollars. A few independent boats sold their salmon at the dock for a $1 a pound. If they were licensed to take their catch directly to a restaurant or market, they'd ask $2 a pound.

Farther upriver around The Dalles, Native Americans—under their treaty rights—could sell hook-caught salmon at any time of the year, usually beginning at $5 per pound. They couldn't use nets except in season, according to *The Daily Astorian* and *The Oregonian*.

I built my boat, *Ann Louise*, named for my wife, in 1988. I designed it, cut it all out of aluminum, and then got a welder to weld it.

Most of the salmon we caught were reds and weighed six pounds. Occasionally, we would get a king salmon, twenty to forty pounds. Different companies wanted fish handled certain ways and wanted different numbers of pounds in their brailers—cargo net bags— usually 500 to 1,000 pounds. Our company didn't care, so we'd put a ton in each of our brailers.

Brailer bags had draw strings at the bottom end so when the boats got to the cannery ships, or to the land canneries, the bags were untied and the fish dropped into the cannery holds where they were then processed for quick freezing or canning.

Ward Cove had all land-based canneries and freezing plants in Bristol Bay, Alaska. Bristol Bay is above the Aleutian Islands and situated adjacent to, but south of, the Bering Sea. Both are part of the Pacific Ocean. Bristol Bay is famous for its fishing.

I last fished at Ekuk, near Dillingham, across from Clark's Point in Bristol Bay. I was glad I had the opportunity to fish there.

Ralph Peitsch and his wife had six children. When Ralph wasn't busy checking out and replacing dock piling with his son, he helped his wife in their store, The Astoria Marine Trading Co., in Astoria, Oregon. Ralph was also known to relate wild fishing tales alongside the Fisher Poets. He is now retired.

"...he could follow my orders,
or I would press charges..."

Ain't No Sunshine
from the book, *Courage*

W. A. "Bill" Johnson

In 1960, I was a non-commissioned officer in the army. I was stationed in Panama and assigned to Combat Support Company, 2nd Battle Group, 10th Infantry. I had started my assignment as a squad leader in Mortar Platoon with seven squad members, an eclectic mix of GIs: Italians, Swedes, Poles, etc. It was a great mix of America, and they got along well together, and I with them. I had no idea that my little piece of heaven would eventually take a drastic change.

In the '60s, there were a large number of blacks coming into the service. They were joining the military for a number of reasons, but I've always felt that one of the main reasons was, that in the '60s, the military was one of the few places a black man could find some semblance of equality and a chance to excel and advance himself.

Please understand, I was close to and loved each and every one of my fellow Non-Coms. I even shared quarters with one of them for a deal of my time on base. However, our feelings on race were miles apart. I was from the North, and had been raised that we are all equal, while a large number of them were from the South, and at the time, that greatly influenced their view of black GIs.

My experience in leading men as well as children is that they tend to live up to your expectations of them.

Since our southern sergeants were unable to view the black recruits as men and equals, there were bound to be conflicts and great difficulties. This led to most of the blacks being labeled with a number of descriptive adjectives: difficult, trouble, uncooperative—just to name a few.

One by one these black soldiers were moved from squad to squad until they came to rest in my squad. There they quickly found out that the color of their skin meant nothing to me. I was only interested in their performance.

Once in my squad, these "difficult," if not "impossible" men became good soldiers. This fact was not lost on my superiors. In short order, one by one, my eclectic mix of America was becoming all black.

In no time at all, there were seven black squad members and me that proved to be the best squad in all of Combat Support Co. I'm giving you this background so that you might be able to appreciate the upcoming irony.

One afternoon, I was assigned as non-com in charge of a detail of men provided for me. Our job was to perform the task that had been assigned. These were normally not choice assignments. The reason for that is, that the work crew was often made up of men from other squads. Common sense tells us that, you aren't going to be sent the best soldier from another Non-Com's squad.

I no longer recall what the detail even was, but I do remember Private Hanley. There were a number of jobs and duties involved, and some of them were less desirable than others. However, each duty had to be performed.

Apparently, Hanley felt the task I had assigned him was particularly unpleasant as he informed me that he wasn't going to do what I was asking. There is no room in the military to allow choice. Therefore, I assured him that he *was* going to fulfill the task at hand.

This brought about the much-used response of

uncooperative blacks at that time. He informed me that I was racially prejudiced against him and only chose him because he was black. Based upon my squad of seven blacks, this charge sent me into a fit of laughter that all but caused me to roll on the floor in hysteria.

No amount of explanation on my part seemed to sway Pvt. Hanley, and that left me with little alternative. I explained to him that he had two choices; he could follow my orders, or I would press charges and have him court-martialed.

This caused Hanley to up the ante. He informed me that he was going to Company Headquarters and report me for racial prejudice. He headed down the stairs for the orderly room with me in tow.

As we hit the bottom floor and were approaching the orderly room, I saw the company's new First Sergeant headed in our direction. At this time, I think it would be relevant for me to point out that, our new First Sergeant was a very black, black man. He stood somewhere between 6'4" and 6'5". I have no idea how much he weighed, but I used to worry that he would get stuck in the doorframes. Believe me when I say, none of this was fat. He was all man and muscle!

When Hanley saw the First Sgt., he picked up speed, and upon arriving in front of the sergeant, proceeded to inform him that I was racially prejudiced, and that he wanted to bring charges against me.

I will never forget what ensued. Hanley had barely spoken the words, when the First Sgt. grabbed him by his lapel, and turning, shoved Hanley up against the wall, then raised him up the wall until the two were eye to eye.

"What color am I?" asked the First Sgt.

"Black, Sergeant," said Hanley, with his eyes widened the size of coke bottles.

"There is no such thing as racial prejudice in my company, do you understand that?" asked the Sergeant.

"Yes, Sergeant," was the reply.

"Then you get your black ass up those stairs, and you

do whatever this sergeant tells you to do. Do you understand me?" he asked.

The reply was a very loud, "Yes, Sergeant!" whereby he was returned to the ground.

Needless to say, I never again had any problem with Pvt. Hanley when our paths had the occasion to cross.

W. A. "Bill" Johnson, graduated from Myrtle Point High School in Oregon, in 1954. Forty years later, single again, he reconnected with Shirley Davenport at a high school class reunion, and they were married a short time later. They are now enjoying spending time with their collective grandchildren and great-grandchildren.

"He had two sister stars, fleas
Midge and Mage."

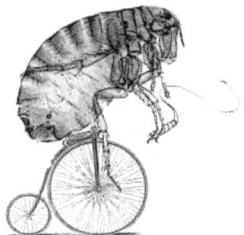

Flea Circuses
Really Do Exist

Phoebe Allen

"You didn't really see a flea circus, did you? You're kidding, aren't you, Mom?" my daughter, Candi, asked incredulously upon my return from Copenhagen, Denmark.

"Yes, Candi, I really did see a flea circus."

In June 1961, as tour chairman, I accompanied a group of federal employees from the San Francisco Bay Area to Europe. We landed in Denmark, and we were all anxious to see an amusement park in Copenhagen called Tivoli.

It was said to be the inspiration for Walt Disney's Disneyland. The park was filled with theatrical shows such as opera, ballet, musical comedy, and drama.

When the other Americans visited a tavern, I stayed with our knowledgeable Danish tour guide. He taught school in the winter and escorted visitors around Denmark in the summer. He took me to an area filled with honky-tonk shows that reminded me of Coney Island.

My curiosity was great as we entered a small room holding a large, round tub where the trained fleas performed with a little help from Madame Cardosa. She was a European lady, the trainer, who used tweezers to help the fleas perform.

Her amazed spectators sat on stools and observed

the show through a huge, round magnifying glass that was passed around. The show opened with miniature chariot races. Tiny shirt buttons served as wheels. High wire acts followed where miniature poles and a chair were used for balancing. Several fleas in costume danced on the high wire.

Even today in memory, I find this spectacular event hard to believe.

Recently, after a sumptuous continental-style meal at Caprials in Portland, Oregon, with my friends Curt and Julia, I reminisced about having seen a flea circus. Julia was a non-believer.

"Unless I see proof on the Internet that there is such a thing as a flea circus, I will not believe it," Julia stated emphatically.

I contacted my other daughter, Jacqui, in Warrenton, Oregon, to help me out by searching the Internet. She complied by providing a stack of printed material and many colored photos on the veracity of the flea circus.

At the time—February 2003—Professor Adam Gertsocov, a trained circus clown from Providence, Rhode Island, had his flea circus at Times Square. The insects entertained every Saturday and Sunday at noon.

Gertsocov was the proprietor of the Home Acme Miniature Circus, the first flea circus to hit Times Square in more than forty years. He had two sister stars, fleas Midge and Mage.

Fleas live for two years and can carry more than 100,000 times their body weight. Gertsocov fed them every two weeks with his own blood. At age thirty-seven, he was a graduate of the University of Pennsylvania and also of the Ringling Brothers Barnum and Bailey Clowns College.

He dressed in what might be called the layered clown look, from purple top hat to red, white, and green shoes. He was the picture of a carnival showman—black silk shirt, bow tie, gold lame vest, magenta corduroy tails, and floppy plaid pantaloons.

Throughout the show, Gertsocov delivered corny jokes and narrated the history of the flea circus. He ended his show with a perilous finale. The fleas were blasted from a cannon through a flaming hoop of fire.

There are said to be only a few flea circuses still running in the world today.

Phoebe Allen was a member of the Lake Oswego Adult Community Center in Lake Oswego, Oregon. She led an exciting life, interviewing many interesting personalities in unique situations and fascinating places. Unfortunately, she failed to interview the fleas.

"...a devastating fire destroyed most of the city..."

Gold Mining Ghost Towns

Ed Hortsch

A Corvair was never meant to be an off-road vehicle. However, such was the role my dauntless Corvair Monza played on many occasions—traveling on roads unintended for *any* type of vehicle.

Perhaps you wonder how I managed to be on such roads in the first place?

Two of my hobbies are seeking out covered bridges and ghost towns, primarily in Eastern Oregon. Covered bridges are often found on back roads, and they are usually paved roads, perhaps not always well maintained, but paved, or at least graveled. Ghost towns, on the other hand, lurk in the less traveled regions of the countryside.

About thirty years ago, I really had no idea just how bad these "roads" could be. One particular trip took me into the region around Baker City. I had often heard of Cornucopia, an old mining town north of Baker City. As I planned my trip, I found there were a number of other vintage mining towns in the area, so I decided to make a loop and see as many as possible.

Cornucopia proved to be interesting and relatively easy to reach. It was about thirty-five miles, as the crow flies, northeast of Baker, or about forty miles east on Highway 86 to Halfway, then north about fifteen miles. Platted in 1886 as a mining town, and abandoned in 1942, there were many old buildings and houses still standing—just no residents. Items were left in place as if the town had been deserted very suddenly. As I looked around, I almost expected to see some old prospector step around the corner.

Bourne was the next town on my list. It was more remote than Cornucopia, nestled in the Elkhorn Mountains about fifteen miles west of Baker—again following a crow—then down a side road north to Sumpter, about six miles. This gravel road was even more difficult to travel. One section was like driving across a giant washboard. I thought the car would rattle apart beneath me! The road finally smoothed out a little before I reached Bourne.

Bourne was like going back in time. Also a mining town, it was established in the late 1880s as Cracker City and populated by 1,500 residents at its peak. It was virtually deserted in the early 1900s. There were just a few abandoned cabins left, but in a most picturesque setting. High mountains provided the appropriate background.

The only way to leave Bourne was by the route I came. It was bad enough to travel the washboard-like road once, but now I had to rattle over it again to reach my next destination.

Back from Bourne, I moved on to Sumpter, another old mining town, but dignified by an ancient gold dredge sitting in the middle of the Powder River. Situated on a large boat that looked as if it were once a ferry, the dredge had several twenty-eight-cubic-foot buckets to scoop up gold-bearing earth or river gravel. The first settlers arrived in the early 1860s and grew to about 3,500 residents in the early 1900s. Mining continued there until a devastating fire destroyed most of the city in 1917. These days, Sumpter is a nice little historic town with a couple hundred residents and a few businesses.

It was lunchtime, so I looked around for a possible place to eat and found Our Place ICHALABA, which stood for: Ice Cream, Hamburgers, Laundry, Bath—a real one-stop shopping center. I ordered and was served an excellent Reuben sandwich. At the counter beside me sat an old cowboy claiming to be three hundred years old. I had my doubts. He was more than willing to yarn anyone who cared to listen, but I wanted to get back on the road.

Turned out, the best was yet to come. I wanted to look over Greenhorn City, which was about fifteen miles west from Sumpter on Highway 7 and farther up into the mountains. After those first fifteen miles, I turned north on a winding, old side road for about another twelve miles. The gravel road turned into an even narrower gravel road, which became an even narrower dirt road.

It was very dry at the time, and the temperature was over 100 degrees. Consequently, it was quite dusty. In spite of the heat, I had the windows rolled up, and still, dust was pouring in through every little crack. The red interior was now brown, as was I. I could hardly see through the windshield for the dust both inside and out. I actually had to turn on the windshield wipers.

I finally arrived at Greenhorn City. It was first populated in the 1860s and shut down in the early 1940s when a federal law made gold mining illegal during WWII. The road formed a circle, and there were a number of old buildings around it—some standing, some collapsed. As I got out of the car, I met the one resident of Greenhorn—an old man who said he was the sheriff, as well as the mayor, justice of the peace, and postmaster.

He noticed something dripping from my car. It was motor oil. I remembered a rather hard bump on the way in. Apparently, a rock punched a hole in the oil pan. Fortunately, I had cans of oil with me, so I removed the filler cap, poured some in, and after bidding farewell to the town's single occupant, I started back down the mountain. I stopped a couple of times to check and add oil before I made it back to the highway, and some distance on down it to the town of Austin.

I was told there was a garage that might be open in

Prairie City. That meant driving another twenty-eight or thirty miles west, and, thankfully, I managed to get there with the car still running! When I arrived in the charming small town by the John Day River, I found the automotive garage, and the mechanic told me he could fix the Corvair by the next afternoon. So, I needed a place to stay for the night.

Across the street, on the corner, stood an old hotel. Though it didn't really look like it was open for business, I went inside and rang a bell on the counter. After a few minutes, a ghostly-looking old man came out from behind a curtain. There was something about him that reminded me of Boris Karloff.

When I got up to my room, I wanted to take a shower immediately to wash off the caked-on brown dust. When I saw myself in the mirror, I realized I could have fit right in to one of the ghostly Karloff monster movie scenes. I must have looked quite a sight to both the mayor of Greenhorn and old man "Boris."

I let the hot water tap run for a few minutes. The water didn't seem to get hot, nor was it really cold either. But, with the day's temperature still as high as it was, a lukewarm shower was refreshing.

I had dinner in the restaurant across from the hotel. It was also a bar, and there was a fellow wandering around the place who just had to be the town drunk. He was still there when I went for breakfast the next morning! By the afternoon, my car had been repaired, and I went on my way, paying much closer attention to road conditions.

Prairie City had about a thousand inhabitants almost thirty years ago, but it has grown since then. So, I hear, have all the ghost towns I explored on my trip. Perhaps the current residents would be offended to have their hometowns referred to as ghost towns. If so, I apologize.

Today, I own a Jeep. And it has yet to be on a rough road.

Ed Hortsch was originally from Portland, Oregon, but lived in Astoria for over a decade. He owned a personable, odd-colored cat named Peaches and worked for the Astoria School District as a school bus driver and head mechanic. His hobbies included singing, photography, collecting and restoring antique office equipment, and collecting Matchbox toys. He also believed in helping at his church.

"Driving down the street in a flashy red convertible came four girls."

A Dry and Dusty Town

Joan Masat

Lads can be such clowns messing around with each other and teasing girls. The leader of the s**t kicking group was Shorty, a good-looking, six-foot-tall goofball.

They were swaggering down Main Street—moved over for three elderly ladies and bowed like great gentlemen. The ladies found it very funny, so they curtsied. The young lads moved on down the dusty sidewalk on that very hot August evening in Central Oregon.

"What do we want to do?" asked Slim.

"I don't know." Shorty yawned. "This town is dead. Here we are on a Saturday night, and I've already seen the movie at the Bijou."

Rick piped up, "Let's go throw rocks in the river."

"No," the others said in unison.

"Besides," Ed added, "it's pretty well dried up in August, it's too hot to walk, and it's gettin' dark."

They all sat down on the bench on the curb outside the barbershop window and sighed.

"Well, we could run through town smashing windows," Shorty suggested.

"That is the dumbest idea you've ever had," snarked Rick with exasperation in his voice, "other than painting black cows' tails red in the middle of the night."

"That was fun," remarked George, "but the hardware store is closed, and I don't think they'll ever sell us any more paint."

Rick, who thought he was the smart one in the group, commented, "But it was a learning experience."

"A what?" asked George. "The only thing we learned was to be careful where we stepped."

"Nothing ever happens in this town," sighed Shorty as he tried unsuccessfully to make music with a blade of grass.

A tumbleweed rolled haphazardly down the street. They looked at it and started to sing "Tumbling Tumbleweed" but soon gave it up, as no one could remember the words.

Then, driving down the street in a flashy red convertible came four girls—high school seniors. They were yelling and laughing, and drinking.

The boys—all sophomores—stood up and put on their best casual look.

When the girls saw the five younger boys smiling at them and trying to look cool, they burst into a fit of laughter, gave them the finger, and rolled on out of town as they threw out a couple of empty beer cans.

The lads yelled various names at the girls and sat back down. Nothing was said for a while—too damn hot.

In just a matter of minutes, the boys heard a siren and saw the flashing lights of the sheriff's car as it sped past—followed shortly by the volunteer fire department.

Without speaking, they all got up and ran down the street after them. An ambulance passed them as they sweated along.

They were all thinking the same thing. *The girls didn't make the turn by the canyon.*

Another police car went by.

They were almost to the canyon when a policeman ran over and stopped them.

He said, "Boys, you don't want to see this! Go home, and stay there. If you know any of the girls and their families, don't call them. Let us take care of this."

Rick asked, "Are they all okay?"

"No, they are not."

It was a long walk back to town. It was dark by then,

and the stars were out with a quarter moon.

The universe was still there—but it had shifted. Something had changed for the five friends, and things would never be the same.

"...my mouth was so dry,
I couldn't speak."

Till the End of Time

Nicholas Emrich

I'll be sixty-six tomorrow. I'm a bachelor. I've never been married. Oh, I'm attracted to women—don't get me wrong. And I admire them. The world would be a better place if women ran it.

But I'm not attracted enough to consider marriage and all its baggage. Not that I wouldn't be faithful. I've been faithful all my life.

Her name was Margaret. I saw her at the beginning of seventh grade. She played flute in the junior high and high school bands. Her father was a minister. I loved her passionately for over five years.

High school had been a total bust. I plotted my days around her classes so I could see her—just see her.

She never noticed me.

She was pretty, yes, but—besotted though I was—even I could recognize other girls as more beautiful. But, there was something about Margaret.

No, I never told her how I felt. Actually, she was going out with another boy. The one time I was accidentally alone with her, my knees knocked, and my mouth was so dry, I couldn't speak.

Because of her, I couldn't concentrate in school. My grades were poor. I finally graduated in summer school.

After high school, I never saw Margaret again. I was fortunate to be accepted at Elmhurst College, a well-regarded institute. I graduated cum laude.

It is true that when I moved out to California twenty

years ago, I did go with a French girl—Francesca—for a while. We almost went to Catalina Island once.

Sadly, she got carsick before we made it to the ferry. We went to Santa Barbara instead. I never did get to see Catalina Island.

Francesca liked to cook, and for supper one night, she made a quiche Loraine and a spinach salad. She poured bacon drippings over the salad.

I was a vegetarian, and she knew it. I was never so sick in my life—for four long days. That was the end of that romance.

So, tomorrow, I'll be sixty-six—and a lifelong bachelor. Dante had his Beatrice. I had my Margaret.

"German planes would fly over—
night after night..."

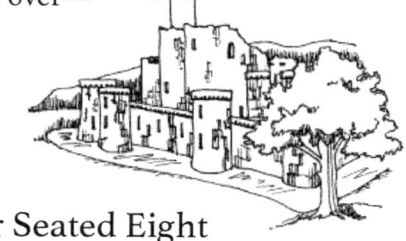

Our Air Raid Shelter Seated Eight

M. Gwanso

The next time I fly over to London, I'm going to fly business class. For ten hours, I muttered this under my breath, feeling more like a sardine every mile. The big compensation was the thought of the train ride to my old stomping grounds in North Wales once I arrived.

What's more, there was a comfortable bed in my grandfather's old bedroom awaiting me—the room where he died seventy years ago. Also, the attached nursery was renovated into a much-needed bathroom.

As children, it was where my sister and I spent our summer holidays, swimming in the Menai Straits and roaming freely all over Beaumaris Castle and its grounds, on the Isle of Anglesey. Happy memories.

My first day there, I walked down Church Street and found a bench by the beach. It didn't take long for the seagulls and jackdaws to spy me. They started swooping and screeching all around in search of some tidbits.

The noise filling the air brought back memories of the winter of 1942. That was when German planes would fly over—night after night—droning overhead toward their main target, Liverpool, England.

Most people today are ignorant of the fact that Ireland was neutral during WWII. We in North Wales, living about sixty miles east of Dublin, were under a strict blackout and could show no lights after dark, whereas all of Dublin was brightly lit.

That allowed the Germans to get their bearings, then

fly eastward, over Wales, to drop their deadly loads on the city of Liverpool and its people. I remember standing on the shore, watching the night sky glowing red, knowing what devastation was being wrought to our east.

My father was a member of the Royal Observer Corp. From their camp up on the mountain, the group of older men monitored the approach and direction of the enemy planes. They would warn the city authorities to set off the air raid sirens.

Further into the war, a few British night fighters became active, and they would intercept the bombers. That's when we became victims of the bombs.

In their eagerness to escape, the German pilots would drop their loads haphazardly. That way, they would lighten their planes and be able to climb higher to avoid our fighters.

One night, North Wales caught two blockbusters. They were the big, powerful bombs. Quite a few women and children were killed.

After that, when the sirens wailed, we would crawl out of bed and drag ourselves into the cold, damp air raid shelter. It was just a slit trench surrounded by sandbags—but it sat eight uncomfortably. The trouble was, we had to swing down into it.

One time as we attempted to go in, the sandbags broke open. Ah, well. What could we do? We just stood outside, watched the searchlights scan the night sky, and listened to booms of the anti-aircraft guns.

Thinking back, I realized that at no time that night did anyone show any fear.

"...we could have ended up dead in a matter of seconds."

Two Buckets in Saudi Arabia

Rick Andriesian

From 1983 to 1988, I worked at the King Faisal Specialist Hospital and Research Center in the capital city of Riyadh, Saudi Arabia. Reportedly, it was the best hospital for 5,000 miles in any direction. I was a registered nurse in the Emergency Department.

Above All, I Didn't Want My Life to Be Ordinary

It all began in 1967. I was fourteen that year when I heard that construction was beginning on the Alaska pipeline. I began to dream of travelling to exotic Alaska to work when I turned eighteen. The adventure and the "big money" that people were earning were exciting to think about.

But, as I began to think about future travel beyond Alaska, I realized I wanted more than the typical American vacation. I wanted to go overseas, learn new languages, meet the people, and learn about their cultures—something out of the comfort zone of most Americans.

Become a Nurse? Are You Kidding Me? I'd Rather Be A Nun

1967 was also the year our home burned to the

94

ground. We were left with the clothes on our backs, and moved in with my grandparents.

A year later, we had built a new home on our family's forty-acre farm. I was fascinated by the design, planning, and building process, and I began to dream of building my own dream house.

In 1969, when I was a sophomore in high school, my father and I discussed many career options. His first suggestion was that I apply to the U.S. Air Force Academy and become a pilot and a carrier officer. That became my number one goal.

My dad was a dentist. I still describe him as the smartest and most talented man I've ever known. He knew several men who were nurses at the our local hospital, and he said, "You ought to think about that."

To humor him, I said, "Sure, Dad, I'll think about it."

But in 1969, what I was really thinking was, *Me, become a nurse? Are you kidding me, dad? I'd rather be a nun!*

At that time, the odds of me wanting to become a nurse were as likely as me wanting to join a nunnery: NO WAY!

Though I didn't want to live a typical American life, I did have a plan as I approached graduation from high school in 1971 in Warrenton, Oregon.

Plan A was to attend the U.S. Air Force Academy— but my less than perfect eyesight killed that plan. So I shifted goals.

Plan B was to attend the U.S. Coast Guard Academy. I got my Congressional nominations, passed the initial screening, and took the scholastic and aptitude tests. I passed all those and went up against the physical. I did fine until the eye exam. They don't require perfect vision, as did the Air Force Academy, but my vision was slightly outside their requirement.

Plan C? I didn't have one. So, instead of starting at the U.S. Air Force or Coast Guard Academy, I graduated and spent the summer mowing grass at the local country club.

With no specific goal, I spent a year at nearby Clatsop Community College in Astoria playing basketball and occasionally studying. I was still mostly without direction, although at the time, I was considering becoming a preacher.

Instead of flying Air Force jets, I spent my second summer after high school gutting and cleaning thousands of salmon a day at the fishing port of Hammond, Oregon.

I read quite a bit in my time off, and I was inspired by one book, *Conscience and Conflict,* by Oregon Senator, Mark Hatfield. It was given to me by one of the leaders of our church, Richard Carruthers. Hatfield had been his roommate at Willamette University.

The book changed my mind. Its premise was that as a Christian, I couldn't expect to be a successful minister to people's spiritual needs if their physical needs of food, shelter, and good health were unmet. *Then* it made sense to become a nurse.

Four years later, in 1976, I graduated from the University of Oregon School of Nursing with a BSN degree, Bachelor of Science in Nursing.

I Had a New Plan

So, I made a new plan. It wasn't very spiritually oriented. I'd get a job and buy a house, then a new car, then some open land in the country. Ultimately, I'd build my dream house in the country and have a family.

Once I had the job, house, car, and bare land, I started looking for an overseas job to pay for the dream house, as well as for the adventure of it.

The only well-paying job I could find was in Saudi Arabia. It paid 9,045 riyals—that was over $2,000 U.S. per month—ten percent more than my nursing salary in a Portland hospital. And it was tax-free!

With Saudi Arabia producing a huge portion of the world's oil, millions of foreign workers went to work there from the 1960s to the 1990s. So, in October 1983, I signed a two-year employment contract and left for Riyadh, Saudi Arabia. I had begun my journey on the road to being "not ordinary."

I was one of twenty-five recruits from the United States and Canada. I flew from Portland, Oregon, to Nashville, Tennessee, for a day and a half of orientation. Classes gave us an overview of Saudi culture and the Muslim religion.

Then, it was on to Atlanta, New York City, and finally, the thirteen-hour flight to Riyadh, the capital of the Kingdom of Saudi Arabia.

Apparently, until the 1960s, Riyadh was a mud-walled city of maybe 10,000 people. Oil money changed that. By 1983, there were a million residents, and it was turning into a major world city.

We arrived late at night. My first daytime view of the city of Riyadh was pretty dreary. From my third floor apartment in the Western men's compound, my first impression was of an incredibly dry, brown, and dusty country.

To the north, I could see dozens of cranes that were the humorously named "national bird." These were ten-story tall industrial cranes, constantly picking up and setting down bricks, steel, and concrete on the hundreds of building sites.

I knew to expect this, but still, the most startling sight was that of men in white tunic-like, ankle-length gowns—thobes—and women in abayas, the long, black cloaks.

We arrived shortly after the oil peak in 1983, when the decline of revenues began. A week later, there was a ten percent devaluation of the currency. I was then earning precisely what I had been in the U.S. But, I still came out ahead, as I had a fully furnished apartment, no utilities, and a free shuttle between the hospital and home. And, I paid no US taxes. My only expenses were food and travel. I entertained myself by using a tape recorder to describe all the unusual things I saw and experienced—and *everything* was new and weird.

Everyone Gets Two Empty Buckets When They Arrive

My second day in the Kingdom, I was invited to a goodbye party in my compound. I asked my new friend, Bill Jackson, why the guy was leaving. Bill was from Paris—that is, Paris, Tennessee, which is not to be confused with Paris, France.

In his southern drawl, he said, "You've got to understand that figuratively speaking, and whether they know it or not, everyone gets two empty buckets when they first arrive here. One bucket is for all the money you hope to make, and the other bucket is for all the crap you have to take while you're here. When either one gets full, it's time to leave. And believe me, it doesn't matter which bucket gets filled up first—whether it's your money bucket or your crap bucket, when the first one gets full, it's time to leave."

I kind of scratched my head at that one. "What?"

He elaborated. "You think about that for a while. Even if you don't get it now, as soon as one bucket is full, you'll know it. And you'll know it's time to go home."

Bill turned out to be right.

I Got Really Good at Hitchhiking

In our hospital of 4,000 employees, there were over sixty different nationalities represented. Staff from thirteen countries worked in the ER. Canadian, American, Lebanese, Yemen, and Sudan. Over half were from the Middle East, and Muslim parts of Africa. The main working language was English.

I was better prepared than most of those in my group were to cope with the many cultural eye-openers, as I had talked with guys who had lived there, and I had seen their slides before my arrival. Also, I had studied the Arabic phrase book beforehand and knew some basic terms. These were especially important, as I worked in the Emergency Department.

Phrases vital to communication in the ER were, "Hello. How are you?" "Are you vomiting?" and of course, "How are your bowel movements?" But these phrases were somewhat less useful in talking to your average Saudi businessman or prince.

Part of the initial excitement of being in Saudi Arabia was that I planned it to be a social experiment for me. I planned to exist in a very un-American way by doing without a car for two years. I didn't even take the free bus to work. I hitchhiked.

In the capital city, I had lots of opportunity to be picked up by people from Egypt, Pakistan, Bangladesh, Lebanon, and, of course, Saudi Arabia. While it was not common in Riyadh, I spent much of my time off hitchhiking around the city.

After being picked up, I'd begin talking with my limited Arabic. "I work at the King Faisal Specialist Hospital. I am a nurse in the Emergency Department. I come from America."

Virtually all the people I met while hitchhiking were friendly and as curious about me as I was about them. Most Saudis I encountered were either Bedouin or "city Saudis." The more modern, usually better educated city folk took pride in having clean, pressed, blindingly white thobes and spotless, shiny cars—usually a Mercedes.

In contrast, the Bedouin lived much as they had for centuries. While most still herded goats and camels, the biggest difference was that they got around the city in white Toyota mini-trucks. Often, there was a camel or a few goats in the back. Their trucks were dusty working vehicles, and their formerly white thobes were stained a dusty brown.

One distinctly negative ride I experienced was with a fiftyish Bedouin man in a white Toyota mini-truck. I began my usual greeting in Arabic, and we drove along, attempting to communicate. He smiled broadly, displaying eight teeth. I smiled back, with substantially more teeth. Apparently, he was impressed.

He was friendly. I was friendly. Then, he became way too friendly when he began to stroke my leg.

I pushed his hand away and hoisted my bag onto my lap, protesting, "Lah! Lah! Lah! Wagef henna." *(No! No! No! Stop here.)* I thanked him and quickly got out of the truck.

I started riding the bus the next day.

Rabies Is a Horrible Way to Die

The most memorable event of my first three months working in the emergency room was when we got a call that a patient with rabies was being transferred from an outlying hospital a thousand miles away. The story was that he was a goat herder from the desert mountains far to the west. There were wolves in that region, and he had been bitten by one three months before. Eventually, he got sick, and they took him to the hospital.

At the hospital, he became very ill. You've probably heard tales of people with rabies foaming at the mouth. It's not so much that they foam, but that the disease destroys their nervous system, and they have lost the ability to swallow, so they drool. People in America rarely get rabies anymore. Hardly anyone in the world gets rabies nowadays.

When the man came to our Emergency Department, his mind was obviously badly affected. He was agitated, he was frightened, and he had no ability to communicate. We had no idea if he was in pain or if he understood anything that was happening around him. He was wild-eyed and clearly in horrible distress.

Everyone was wearing gowns and gloves, with head covers and shoe covers. We were all fearful of him because we didn't know how contagious rabies could be. And, we didn't know how to help him. Actually, there was no way to help. He was doomed.

He quickly went from bad to worse. He died a couple of hours after he arrived. I doubt if there are more than ten people in the United States—that's one per thirty-three million Americans—who have seen a person die from rabies. It's a very ugly death!

You get a little nervous after seeing that sort of thing. I did some research about rabies the next day, then took the full series of shots. Despite all the protective gear, and no known direct exposure, I didn't want to take any chance of contracting the deadly virus.

We Had a Murder in the ER

Men and women are very segregated in Saudi society. Even among Western employees, they had single men's apartment compounds five miles from the hospital. Of course, single Western women were housed in apartments at the hospital where they could be watched and kept "safe."

There was no interaction between Western men and Saudi women. If any guy got a glimpse of the face of a beautiful Saudi woman and was crazy enough to want to get involved with her—well, his life would be in peril if any attempt were made. Transcultural relationships couldn't even be imagined.

Sometime in 1987, in my fourth year in Saudi Arabia, I experienced the most shocking incident of my ten-year career as a nurse. Thirty years later in 2017, it is *still* the most shocking event I've ever experienced.

Moments after I got to the ER to start a routine night shift, a Filipino man was brought in with an "amputated" penis. He had been caught by a Saudi man, fooling around with the guy's sister. The man was forced to drink gasoline and then had his penis cut off.

He was unconscious and bleeding profusely. We stabilized him, quickly took him to the operating room, and left him with the surgical team. Minutes later, the surgery nurse appeared, as pale as a ghost, and told us the Egyptian plastic surgeon had been murdered.

I went pale and was as shaken as she was.

The surgery nurse related the story. They had put the Filipino man on the operating table but didn't restrain him. Apparently, he didn't have enough anesthesia, and he woke up in horrible pain in the middle of the surgery.

He looked around at all the scary, masked people surrounding him and grabbed the first weapon he saw— a very sharp pair of surgical scissors. He stabbed the surgeon at least ten times in the head. The doctor immediately dropped dead.

Six weeks later, the policeman in charge that night was back on other business and said, "Ah, I remember you. You were here the night the surgeon was killed in the ER."

I asked, "What happened to the guy who killed the surgeon?"

"Well, they took him to jail right away, then to court, where he was tried and quickly convicted. He was executed about a week after he killed the doctor."

I supposed that was what the law required. It definitely left me shaking. I still feel goosebumps and get half-nauseous whenever I tell that story.

I Was Considered a Ladies' Man

I was in nursing school from June 1974 to December 1976. There were 190 women and only ten men in my class. I enjoyed that. I joined the medical school fraternity Phi Beta Pi. In a twenty-four-bedroom frat house a block from the school, there were twenty-two medical students, one dental student, and myself, the only nursing student.

Our Latin motto was "Custodiae Virginatus," meaning "Guardians of Virginity." I'm not sure if that was true for all my frat brothers, but since I was what they called a late bloomer, it was true for me.

Beginning in the 1960s, Western women working at the hospital had occasionally been allowed inside the Western men's compounds for parties on the weekends.

That was fun while it lasted.

After I'd attended only one co-ed party, the privilege was cancelled nationwide just two weeks after I'd arrived in Saudi Arabia. Wow! I guess I had more of a reputation as a ladies' man than I thought.

I can't prove it, but I like to think that my Casanova charms were personally responsible for changing the laws of an entire nation, and for preserving the virtue of Western women in Saudi Arabia for generations to come.

Just kidding. I know my limitations—but just saying it jokingly is good for my fragile male ego.

There Was an Art to Driving a Hard Bargain

At first, I had a lot of enthusiasm for meeting the people and learning the culture. However, I eventually realized that for a country boy from Oregon, living in a city with no way out led to insanity. My great social experiment of going carless for two years was taking its toll on me.

No matter where in the world I chose to live, I needed frequent access to the countryside. In the extremely restrictive country of Saudi Arabia, that need was even more apparent.

So, after six months of living in the Kingdom, I decided I had to get a car. I went down to the local Daihatsu dealer. I had never heard of the brand before, but people I knew recommended it as the best 4x4 desert vehicle. After looking at several models, I decided a Daihatsu Jeep was what I wanted.

I asked about financing.

"Financing? Oh. You just bring in all of the money."

In other words—strictly cash.

I decided to negotiate. After half an hour, we arranged for me to put $6,000 down and provide the balance in two easy payments of $1,200 a month. That was my "financing."

A few days later, I went to the bank, got $6,000 in Saudi riyals, and put it in a large brown paper bag. It was nearly full. I took the money across town to the Daihatsu dealer, very tightly clasping the bag in my lap. To my knowledge, I was one of the first, if not *the* first one in Saudi Arabia, to get new car financing.

Beware of the Grim Reaper

Driving in the Kingdom was different. For me, it was occasionally amusing, sometimes scary, and on several occasions—horrifying. Lots of money distributed by Saudi royals to the common people meant lots of high end Mercedes Benz sedans, almost certainly more per capita than anywhere else in the world. However, having no drivers education meant no one seemed to consider safety, rules, or courtesy.

Saudi drivers seemed to think there was no reason to follow the laws—since no one else did. Speed was king, along with an aggressive attitude. "I'm important, so get out of my way," was the rule of the day.

Throughout the city, there was construction being done on highways, high-rise buildings, sewers, and water distribution systems. A friend of mine witnessed how "slowing down" while driving around a detour was executed by a local driver.

A Mercedes going up a five-lane city street passed him at about 100 miles an hour. The driver didn't see the construction signs, went through a barrier, and sailed across a thirty-foot wide, forty-foot deep chasm.

With no stuntman ramp, the car fell a few feet short of successfully jumping the gap. Instead, it nearly impaled the dirt like an arrow then dropped to the bottom of the abyss. The driver didn't survive.

I Became the "Ugly American"

After several months of driving in the city and experiencing the culture, the honeymoon was over. I'd had enough. I generally had pretty good manners, but I got so every third word out of my mouth was a slur, a vulgarity, or worse. Whenever I saw an ill-mannered Saudi driver, I would flip him off. I had never flipped anyone off before in my life.

One day, I was driving down a five-lane road, and all the traffic stopped at a stop sign. I was in the left-hand lane, planning to make a left turn.

Four lanes to my right was a shiny, new Mercedes sedan. When the light turned green, it took off and turned left, crossing all four lanes so it was in the lane with me, nearly causing an accident for everyone between us.

I flipped the bird. Not a little bird. It was the California condor—the largest and most offensive of all the middle fingers ever waved. For at least ten seconds, I was driving with one arm, my head, and half of my chest out the window. I continued waving and yelling in two languages, using all the bad words I knew at least twice.

Seconds later, when I thought the episode was over, I looked up just in time to see the $50,000 Mercedes beside me, then swerving toward me. Fear replaced anger. I dodged it, slowed down, and briefly thought that maybe it would drive off after having "taught me a lesson." I was wrong.

I saw it coming back to complete the job. The car sideswiped me at forty-five miles per hour, nearly forcing me onto the curb. Finally, we came to a stoplight 300 yards up the road.

I thought I could make a U-turn to get away from the maniac, but no—there was a car stopped in front of me. Retrospectively, I wish I had gone into four-wheel drive up and over the curb. Unfortunately, I didn't think that fast at the time.

In the Mercedes were four young Saudi men— probably in their twenties—none of them very big, maybe 120 to 140 pounds each. But there were four of them! They were very properly and neatly dressed, riding in the shiny, expensive auto. Apparently, they had too much money.

Their car was right beside my car as we waited for the light to change. I was becoming even more nervous. Suddenly, two of them got out and strode aggressively toward my window. I rolled it down an inch.

"What do you mean waving the finger at us?" they yelled. "We know what that means. What do you mean doing that?"

The two guys stood there while a third guy climbed into my passenger seat. It didn't look good for me.

I took action—shoved the guy out of the passenger seat and slammed and locked that door. In the meantime, a third guy had climbed through the back door of my Jeep where I had some four-foot-long pieces of one-inch steel rebar on the floor. He grabbed a piece and got out.

The first two guys kept jawing at me on the driver's side and didn't seem too threatening. Then, I saw the third guy swinging the rebar like a baseball bat.

First, he hit the bumper and the headlights on my car—my new car! Then, he came around to my side and swung it at my windshield. I ducked, it cracked, I bailed out of the jeep to safety, and then I stood up.

Surprisingly, all four of them took off like scared rabbits. I'm six-foot-two, so maybe they thought I was chasing them—but I was actually ducking so as not to get hit with the rebar.

When the light changed, I picked up the rebar and all the debris, threw it in the back of my Jeep, got in, and took off like a scared rabbit myself. Talk about road rage reform! I have never flipped off anyone else.

There Were Religious Police and a Large Royal Family

The Kingdom was supposedly the home of pure Islam, of the Wahabi sect, which was very conservative, very traditional. So they had their army, their national guard, and they had their regular police.

They also had their religious police, called the mutawa. These were usually older men who had some formal training in religious requirements of the Wahabi sect. Their job was to go around town looking for people who were breaking the rules or laws. It was all about following the rules.

During each of the five prayer times throughout the day, if your shop wasn't promptly closed, they would come in and give you a hard time, possibly even put you out of business.

If you were a woman, Western or otherwise, and not properly dressed—if you didn't have at least your head covered, or weren't wearing a long enough skirt to cover your ankles—they would harass you, or beat you around the ankles with their long canes, or arrest you, or all three.

King Khalid ruled from 1975-1982. During this period, the Kingdom grew and modernized due to increased oil prices—especially after the 1973 oil crisis—and increased wealth.

The Royal Family was very fertile, and everybody had ten kids, so within several generations, there were thousands of princes and princesses. By 1988, there were around 5,000 princes and 5,000 princesses in the Kingdom.

They all had at least a $1,000,000, or allowances. It seemed like it was an incredible waste of financial resources, although the Royal Family did distribute a lot of the money to the people.

Osama bin Laden was born in Saudi Arabia. Raised in the center of the Muslim universe, he learned to hate Western values, America, and the corrupt Saudi Royal Family.

Interestingly, the Royal Family heavily supported the conservative Muslim hatemongers like Osama bin Laden, while being very western.

The irony is that the chickens have come home to roost, because while they supported fundamentalism, they had terrorists plotting against their kingdom—and against the corruption in the Kingdom.

The Saudis Inflicted Justice with a Swift Sword

While I was living in Riyadh, I witnessed a beheading. It was at once both one of the most amazing and disturbing experiences of my life. Not because I enjoyed the gore, the bloodshed, or the circus atmosphere—though there were all those things. It was because it was a surreal, almost magical experience.

Regardless of whether one is in favor of capital punishment or is opposed to it, some countries are going to continue to allow it in their law. Murder, rape, and blasphemy were the main crimes for which Saudi law mandated death.

If you were convicted of murder, beheading was the prescribed method of execution. If you were convicted of theft, the penalty was to have your right hand cut off. Some people see that as barbaric, cruel, and unjust. In Saudi Arabia, it was prescribed in the Koran, and they viewed it as a case of the punishment fitting the crime.

A "bad" beheading is evil, heinous, and designed to horrify. But a proper beheading is a death that is instantaneous and merciful.

Excitement ran high that day. A public beheading had been announced, and the crowd was heavy. It seemed to me that was the Saudi equivalent of the Super Bowl—the biggest event of the year.

There was no stadium, so it was standing room only at "Chop Chop Square." You couldn't stoop down and pick up something because the crowd was packed so tightly. Sometimes when the crowd surged, you were briefly lifted off your feet.

Hundreds of policemen formed a semicircle about fifty feet from the bottom steps of the Justice Building, which was about 500 feet across the square from the largest mosque in the city. Reports were that Westerners were often pushed to the front of the crowd. That's what happened to two of my friends and me. It was kind of scary.

We, and the 10,000 or so "fans," stood in the 100-degree heat of that late morning in August. For forty-five minutes, nothing happened. Then, the police parted the crowd to allow a large, black police van to drive to "center stage."

A few minutes passed before two police officers got out, escorted a prisoner to the base of the steps, and had him kneel between them. The prisoner appeared to be heavily sedated.

Another few minutes passed, and we wondered, *Where's the executioner? What happens next?* It was said that generations of the same family had carried out the role of the royal executioner.

Then, the executioner appeared. He was dark-skinned, tall, and very powerfully built. He wore a turban and a long, flowing desert robe. His face was covered so that only his eyes showed, and he carried a heavy, four-foot-long sword. He must have stepped out of the van, but I blinked and missed the moment of his arrival. It was as if he'd appeared in a cloud of smoke.

The prisoner was kneeling, head hung down, and the two policemen hadn't moved from his side. In a very precisely, choreographed manner, the swordsman quickly strode three steps forward while drawing his sword arm up and back.

At the last moment, the policemen poked the prisoner in the ribs with a stick and got out of the way. The stuporous prisoner responded by straightening his back and neck to look around. The swordsman deftly swung the blade down, pivoted, took three deliberate steps away from the prisoner, and then vanished. The man's head had been cleanly severed in one blow, and the head and body fell—in different directions.

The executioner was in view for less than a total of fifteen seconds. It was like a lethal magic show, but there was no puff of smoke. He must have come and gone from inside the police van.

The prisoner's head and the body were removed immediately, and the crowd began to thin. A few men spit contemptuously in the large pool of blood glistening on the stones. The few women who had dared to appear in public for such an event—even though they were covered from head to toe—were poked, prodded, and pinched black and blue for their temerity for being there.

I Had My Own, Personal Near-Death Experience

The scariest experience I had in Saudi Arabia wasn't the beheading, nor the murder in the ER, nor having the windshield of my car bashed in during my road rage incident. What happened one night out in the desert topped them all.

I ended up living in Saudi Arabia from 1983 to 1988— five full years. During that time, I dated a woman from Michigan. We really hit it off. After a couple of years though, we broke up, but we were still good friends.

She went on vacation and came back after three weeks. We were going to catch up on where she'd been and what she'd been doing. This was risky, because in Saudi Arabia, unless they're married or related, it's illegal for a man and a woman to be together without a chaperone. So, I suggested we go out to the desert.

It was a nice cool evening, and we decided to take a chance. I put a couple folding chairs in the Jeep, and off we went. We drove out of the city so we could look at the stars while we talked.

We travelled a few miles across the flat terrain from the end of a dirt road—about twenty miles from the city. It was close to midnight, and we hadn't seen another light or sign of life in four hours. Our romance was over, but we had a nice time catching up.

Then, off in the distance, we saw the lights of a car coming our direction. We got a little nervous. The car got closer and closer, and it turned out to be our worst fear—the Saudi police. They drove past us a couple hundred yards down the road then turned around.

We saw their lights coming right toward us. We knew we were going to be scrutinized. It was scary for a couple of reasons. What we were doing was illegal—an unmarried man and an unrelated woman unaccompanied in a car—let alone being out together in the desert. In the Saudi culture, that could mean only one thing—we were having sex, and that was forbidden.

It was especially scary because a buddy of mine had left a box of his stuff in my Jeep a few days earlier, and as they pulled up, it crossed my mind that my friend smoked pot—a really stupid thing to do in Saudi Arabia. I didn't have any idea what was in his box. It could've been drugs. It could have been marijuana. It could have been pornography. It could have been all sorts of things that could have gotten me fifty years in prison.

We'd heard stories of foreigners being stopped by police in the desert. The man would be shot and thrown over a cliff. The woman would then be raped, shot, and thrown over the cliff, too—neither of them to be heard from again. There was a cliff just a hundred yards to our right, and I was shaking like a leaf. I'm sure my friend was too.

The two Saudi policemen came up to our window. It was pitch dark except for the car lights behind them. One of them looked very professional and pleasant, a very thin man who spoke some English. With his little bit of English and my little bit of Arabic, we communicated.

His partner stood behind him. He was very small, very slight, maybe weighing 110 pounds at most. He looked angry and suspicious, with a drawn, ferret-like face. He looked like he wanted to hurt someone. He stayed in the background. He apparently didn't speak English.

The first officer asked, "Is this woman your wife? Is she your sister?"

I said, "No."

"You know you can't be out here like this."

"I know, but we're just friends, and we were just talking. Now we're on our way back to the hospital where we work."

"Do you have drugs with you? Do you have any alcohol with you? Do you have any pornography with you?"

I smiled weakly and answered, "Oh, no, no. Of course not."

He then proceeded to look in the back of the car. That was when I was totally shaking because I no idea what was in my buddy's box. Finally, the officer seemed satisfied there was nothing illegal there.

Next, I could tell he wanted to ask something, but he didn't know how to say the word or know how to express it in gestures. It turned out what he wanted to know was if the woman and I, who were not married, were out in the desert having sex. It's a totally foreign concept in Saudi Arabia that a man and a woman could have a friendship not involving sex. We weren't doing anything of the sort. I didn't have to lie about that—or anything else, for that matter.

It became apparent that although he didn't know how to say it, it was critical to his decision making in what was going to happen to us. Once I understood what he wanted to know, I did a certain hand gesture—one finger inserted into a fist, then in and out in a crude manner.

I asked in Arabic, "This? Are we doing this?"

He responded, "Yes, are you doing any of that?"

I answered, "No, no, no." I was smiling and almost laughing at this point. I reassured him, "Oh, no, we would never do anything like that!" And we hadn't.

He seemed satisfied and greatly relieved. He even smiled a little as he said, "Okay, you should go home now, but don't come out in the desert together again."

At this point, his angry-faced partner looked disappointed he wouldn't get to hurt us.

I quickly said, "Yes, sir. We will never do this again. Thank you, and Allah bless you."

We drove back into town very slowly, very carefully, and we were totally shaken. My friend was also totally relieved, because the same things had been running through her mind as had been going through mine—we could have ended up dead in a matter of seconds.

I Had Nearly Filled My Two Buckets

My money bucket never seemed to be even half full. But, many times during my tenure in Riyadh, my crap bucket was nearly full. In October 1988, I had finished my fifth year at the hospital. Things were okay, but I was overdue to sign my next year's contract.

An hour into my shift one night, a friend from the X-ray department came down the hall in tears. One of her Saudi patient's relatives had verbally assaulted her.

"You Americans! Your magazines, your movies, and your ideas! You're ruining my country!" He'd gone on and on until she was in tears.

I became enraged at the nerve of this man taking out all his anger on the sweet young lady who had nothing to do with any of it.

As I was preparing to stomp down the hall to confront him, I asked her, "Who is he? Where is he? What does he look like?"

She was still in tears but answered, "I don't know his name or where he went, and I don't remember what he looked like now."

I took off running toward her department. I don't know what I would have done if I had found the guy, but it would have gotten ugly. I'm sure I would have been thrown in jail.

I suddenly stopped after I'd made it about fifty feet down the hall. I realized I was in a murderous rage, and I was dangerously out of control. If you've ever burned with rage, you know it is emotionally and physically exhausting. I was so very tired.

As I walked back towards the ER, it suddenly dawned on me. *My bucket's full.*

And just like my friend, Bill, had said, "You'll know when it's time to go," I knew. That was my moment of clarity.

It took a few days for me to sort through my thoughts and realize what it meant. *Yes. It's time to go.*

It was five years and four days into my stay. I had long planned how to make a noticeable statement when I left Saudi Arabia. I had a beard and stylishly long hair. No one there had ever seen me close shaven or in a coat and tie.

On my next day off, I went to the barbershop and told the barber in Arabic, "I want all my hair cut off."

He asked, "Kulu?" *(All of it?)*

I answered, "Kulu."

Still unsure, he repeated, "Kulu?"

I smiled, nodded, and gestured emphatically as I repeated, "Kulu, kulu."

Finally convinced, he laughed out loud and hollered excitedly, "Kulu, Kulu!" He knew just what I wanted, and in no time, he'd done what I'd asked.

I snuck back into the men's compound. I didn't want anyone to see me. I shaved my beard off and got out my dress jacket, slacks, shirt, and dress shoes.

It was my day off, but I went into the hospital fifteen minutes before the start of the day shift. I was going to turn in my resignation. I had written a two-page letter describing the incident that led to my decision.

I walked into the Emergency Department wearing my suit, with no hair on my head, no beard on my face. I didn't say anything to anyone—I just smiled and nodded at several people who knew me well.

I went into the locker room. The head of the department walked by but clearly didn't recognize me.

As he passed me, I said, "Good morning, Frank."

He did a double take. "Rick?"

I kept on walking to the head nurse's office. I didn't

walk in. I stayed just out of sight.

I reached inside the door, knocked, and queried, "Mary, are you in?"

She answered, "Yeah," and I walked in.

Mary saw me. She didn't recognize my face, but she recognized my voice. She asked, "Rick? What happened?" as she looked at me in amazement.

"Not much. Just—here's my letter of resignation."

Remember those two buckets? The money bucket never did get full—but the moment I submitted my resignation, my bucket of crap was suddenly empty. I was going home!

Rick Andriesian left Saudi Arabia in November of 1988. He landed in Nepal and began a long-planned around-the-world bicycle tour. He returned to the US, in December 1989, a wiser and better man for having traveled, and for having lived in the Kingdom.

Rick bought his land in the country and built his dream house...but not until after he married and raised and launched two boys into adulthood. He and his wife moved into their new house in 2010, and they are living there happily ever after.

"...I had seen many wonders,
and this was truly one of them."

Secret in the Jungle

Sandra K. Taylor

I headed for the ladder to disembark. I was anxious as I stepped over debris from the large tree limb the boat had snagged in the night.

I was filled with a sense of sadness as well, anticipating the pain and suffering I was about to see. I had heard or read rarely of Hansen's Disease—also known as leprosy—yet had vivid recollections of photos I'd seen of lepers in magazines and medical books.

I walked on a narrow wooden path through a small, poor, dirty little village along the Amazon River. It was a particularly rainy day. When it rains along the Amazon, it is a heavy rain.

Considering everything, the hospital was a fairly nice-looking old wooden structure. It was uncomfortably large, but I was pleasantly surprised by the very warm welcome.

The staff consisted of a nurse and local helpers. The furnishings were sparse and inadequate. The medical and comfort supplies were even more scarce. The structure presented more of a homelike atmosphere than the sterile, regimented environment I had prepared for.

As I walked slowly through the halls and rooms, I was greeted warmly—according to ability—by the patients. There were so many, I wondered where they had all come from.

I was overcome by a cool sensation permeating my

body. I tried to keep my brain intact, but I was being flooded by emotions ranging from love to fear, and everything in between. The pictures from my past reading came alive.

I was being hugged by people with no hands, touched by people with horrible, scaly skin and lesions. I felt weak and overwhelmed. I really wanted to run.

One lady who could only feel me with partial limbs kept repeating the same phrase over and over to me. She spoke into my face. She had no eyes.

I asked the nurse what she was saying with such passion.

"Praise the Lord, you have finally come to save us..." were her haunting words.

I watched as the nurse gave her one of the few aspirin I had brought with me, to melt on her tongue. Fortunately for them, I struggle with severe headaches and had my usual extra supply. But it seemed so meager, as did my own physical disability.

I passed into a larger community room and was totally awestruck to see tables of wonderful stitchery done by these beautiful people with no fingers and little or no hands or eyes.

A man sat on the back porch steps. He held a chisel in the creases of his stomach. He used what he had left of his hands and feet to hold the wood as he flexed his muscles to make beautiful carvings.

I watched in disbelief. As a world traveler, I had seen many wonders, and this was truly one of them.

When I walked back through the village, the rains had stopped. The local children—with their swollen bellies—grabbed onto my hands, grinned, and jabbered. They welcomed me into their world, and I loved them.

As I walked down to the river, I was thinking of all the reasons I had come to the jungle.

I came to see the trees—the bountiful trees. I came to see the animals—the abundant animals. I came to see the people—the beautiful people. I came to see the river—the great river.

I discovered a secret tucked away in the jungle—an uncomfortable secret.

I left the Amazon with my spirit renewed and my values challenged. I felt good, very good.

Sandra K. Taylor is an avid traveler who prefers the wilds of the world to the comforts of convention. Trips to the Amazon, Yangtze, Galapagos, and Serengeti are some of the highlights of her travels. She strives to leave every place she visits and everyone she meets better in some way. She reaps the pleasures of, and accepts the burdens for, the stewardship of this wonderful world. Having been raised in the Midwest, she now calls the Northwest her home. She has been writing since she was very young.

"...I snuck up closer and nabbed him under the net."

Frog Festival

Lorin Weekly

That magic summer when I was ten, Grandpa Lorin and Grandma DeEtte took me fishing at Diamond Lake. Early the first morning, I heard a loud croak, croak, croak!

I struggled out of my sleeping bag and went to search out who the croaker was. Sitting there singing on the lake bank was a great big green bullfrog.

I snuck up on him, but instead of leaping into the water, he dove down a deep hole. Fifty feet down the bank, another croaker began.

I grabbed the landing net and crept after him. He was sitting on a little rise, so I snuck up and nabbed him under the net. I picked Old Croaker out and held him up. He was about nine inches from his head to his frog flippers. He didn't try to hop away and just sat in my hands and croaked.

I put him down on the ground and stroked him. Still, he croaked. He seemed to enjoy the attention. I picked him up again, and he continued singing. I tossed him in the water, where he floated around a bit in a slow frog stroke then shot off like a torpedo to a mallet-shaped log. It was waterlogged, and the handle stuck down four feet through the water and deep into the sand. Old Croaker sat on the mallet head and sang some more.

A slightly bigger bullfrog crawled out of the water and joined him in the chorus. They kept croaking until a third and then a fourth choir member joined them. All faced the strange, quiet beast on the shore. They continued to croak until there were fourteen green and mottled fat frogs crowded together on three feet of log, singing.

A fifteenth bullfrog appeared and elbowed its way on. The mallet log swayed in the waves. As the riders watched, a new buddy showed off in a logrolling contest on an abandoned milk carton he was trying to board.

Finally, managing to get on, he sat to sing. The box rocked and rolled, but he stayed amidships until his boat rammed the log. Half a dozen others took turns joining him.

The gallon milk carton flipped them off a couple at a time. It finally disappeared when too many bullfrogs climbed on. The spout had rolled to a bottom position, and the carton filled and sank.

The frogs on the carton delighted in being dunked. Everyone on the log became hysterical—hiccupping quick, excited croaks. The carton floated several inches below the surface, and each bullfrog dove down to investigate.

One smaller frog got through the spout and came out with salvaged garbage. The carton was a gold mine, loaded with trash, and the smaller frogs took turns with the salvage operation. Another spotted guy drug out a paper napkin that split, dumping its contents of Velveeta cheese.

Before the cheese hit bottom, thirteen watchers leapt off the log and joined in the raid. The smallest frog got only a taste, so it went back to the carton to continue salvaging.

At the frenzied height of the Velveeta cheese to-do, an early morning motorboat shot around the curve of the lake. Instantly, every bullfrog vanished.

The show was over. The strange, quiet beast on the shore smelled Grandpa's coffee and went in search of breakfast.

"Changes are sometimes
for the best in the long run."

The Quintessential
Fixer-Upper

Merielena Johnson

We were living with Dan's folks until our wedding, but the house wasn't very large, and we felt we were in the way. We really wanted a home of our own, but we didn't have a lot of money to work with.

I was fixing my hair in the bathroom one Sunday when Dan called, "Hon, come look at this!" He sounded excited.

I went in and curled up on the bed beside him to read *The Clatskanie Chief* housing ads.

"Look at this one. We might be able to afford it. It's under $100,000. We should at least go check it out."

I was kind of excited too. "Call the number," I said.

"There are two numbers. Which one shall I call?"

"Whoever's home."

Dan knew the area—up in the hills north of Clatskanie, Oregon, about seven miles. It took only a little time to locate the house. It was set back about 500 yards from the county road. It looked good.

"There's moss on the roof, and a couple panels missing in the garage door," I said as we started up the road to the house.

"The ad said it needed work. I like the location. It's a big house. Looks like it has potential. I guess we'll have to see what it's like inside. I'll need to check the foundation and the plumbing too."

"At least the neighbors aren't right up close. We'd have privacy. I'm pretty sure they couldn't see directly in through our windows."

I had a bug about privacy.

The front door was cracked open, and as soon as we pulled up, someone opened the door wide and invited us in.

"You must be the Grants. I'm Alice. We've been living here three years, and we'll be moving the end of January. I'll show you around and answer any questions you have."

Inside, the first thing I noticed was her kids lying on the carpet, watching TV. They didn't say anything or bother to get up—seemed a bit unmannerly. The second thing was the droopy curtains hanging from broken brackets. The room smelled of dog and maybe of mold.

We did like the size of the living room. Its layout pleased us. We especially liked the real wood of the knotty pine paneling.

Just then, Alice's husband came in, dangling a cigarette from his mouth. He did say, "Hi," but I didn't like the cigarette. He seemed a little on the greasy side.

Alice stepped to an archway on the east side of the living room. "I use this little den for an office."

The room had a broken window inside above a desk that was hooked into the wall. A raw hole was cut through the far wall into the next room.

Maybe it has possibilities—but it needs to be redone from scratch.

We followed Alice into the kitchen. It was spacious with lots of cabinets, but it wasn't very clean—and it needed new flooring. A chip was off a corner of the Formica counter, and the stained spots on the white background looked really dirty.

The trash compacter didn't work, the stainless steel sink was cloudy, and the faucet dripped. The dishwasher was so filthy when I looked inside, that it was scary. But we could see the possibilities.

The dining room was a step down from the kitchen. I

liked the brick wall on the south side. It had a built-in bench that needed a good scrubbing—along with everything else. The room was small, and the window had a bullet hole patched with tape in the upper corner. The wallpaper was dark with brown fruit baskets.

The downstairs bedroom, off the dining room, was larger than average—but socks, shoes, dirty clothes, and a badly stained carpet were what hit us in the face.

Also, the family teenager was sleeping—in the mid-afternoon—smelling slightly of alcohol, and strongly of sweat. He was not a pretty sight.

The furnace closet door fell off when Alice opened it. Dirt, fuzz balls, dead batteries, bullets, wadded-up used filters, and general debris filled the space around the furnace. Dan noticed there was no working filter actually in place.

The Venetian blinds were bent, revealing beer cans and empty shotgun and twenty-two shells on the sills, below smeared windows.

On to the bathroom. Again, we liked the space—there were double sinks. But the toilet was leaking, and there were green streaks in the dirty shower. The linoleum was in bad shape.

Dan opened up the sink cabinets and noted dry rot. "The piping will have to be replaced," he said out loud.

We only spent a few minutes in the bathroom and then followed Alice as she opened a door to the shop, which was off the garage. The door was broken, but at least it would shut.

The shop area was a mess. There was a hole in the ceiling sheetrock where the teenager had been exploring the attic and crashed through. License plates were tacked up all over the walls. Parts of a low-built bubble Chevy truck from the '60s were lying about.

Alice said, "When the truck's fixed, it can pull my horse. That's one of the reasons we're moving—there's more land for my horse."

Later, we found out that most of the fifteen acres they'd bought was marshland and under water all winter. Her poor horse barely had enough room to stand on the hillside scrunched against the fence.

"What about the upstairs?" I asked.

"Come on, I'll show you," she said, and led the way—her kids following.

Their bedrooms were upstairs, and they wanted to keep an eye on us.

We walked on a very worn, yellowish carpet covering the stairs. A big room was on the left.

"Honey, look at the view!" I exclaimed. "We can see the river." It was a cloudy day, or we could have seen the hills beyond too.

I knew if we moved here, I'd have to get curtains up fast because I could see into the neighbors' house across the road, even though they were almost a quarter of a mile away. I really freaked out about privacy—especially at night when I'm changing. Maybe it was because I played basketball a lot, and sometimes the dressing areas were not too secure.

There were little windows about ten by thirty-six inches in size on either side of the room where the roof sloped. It was nice to be able to see trees to the north and a kind of good view to the south too.

The carpet was a burnt orange, Berber texture. Maybe they hadn't noticed, but I couldn't miss that there was crap on the north side and cat poop on both sides.

I said to myself, *How gross. How disgusting!*

"There's no closet," I noted to Dan.

Alice said, "We use the shelf in the space under the eaves and a chest of drawers to keep our stuff in."

That didn't sound good to me. I worked downtown and wore dresses a lot. But even though the room didn't have a closet, or even a door, the size was great.

In the hall, I looked up and noticed out loud, "Dan, the whole upstairs has that spray-on plaster sparkle on the ceiling. I hate that stuff. It's really ugly. We had it in a house we lived in when I was little. Dad scraped it all off. This is just as bad. We'll have a lot of scraping to do here, too. And we'll have to do something about a closet.

I have a lot of clothes to hang up."

"Now, hon, don't worry about little things. We'll think about them later," he answered.

We followed Alice across the hall into her little boy's room. He followed us with his airplane—but he wasn't being pesky—just keeping watch.

The first thing I noticed was that the door had a couple holes in it. The wall behind it had a big ding where the knob hit.

The navy blue carpet was filthy and had a lot of dark oil spots, too. It apparently hadn't been vacuumed for weeks—probably months.

Out one window on the roof was a kitty litter box. Surrounding the box, the roof was littered with more poop as well as moss.

Dan looked at the chimney in the closet. "We'll have to do something about this," he stated, poking at the chunks of stuff that had fallen from the cracks. "And we'll definitely need to replace the roof on this side," he added.

It sounded like Dan was beginning to think about the house as if he already owned it, and I knew when Dan decided on something, his mind was usually made up. I could tell he really liked the house—despite its awful condition. The large spaces available and the floor plan pleased both of us.

Over four years earlier, Dan and I met and started going together. We'd only been living together less than a year—but I knew that for something big like a house, I'd let him make the final decision as long as I had input and felt comfortable.

It was obvious we both liked the house, and we followed Alice into the final bedroom. It had a fake wall between it and the half bath. We had missed seeing the bathroom because its door was open. The seat was up on the blue toilet, which was disgustingly dirty. The sink was filthy, too. A loose hangar lay on the floor of the little bathroom closet. The whole room was gross.

It was the smallest bedroom, and had a light blue

shag carpet. This was the little girl's room, and it was cleaner than any of the other rooms.

On a clear day, you could see the volcano, Mount St. Helens, up in Washington State, out the east window. There was a hole in that window the size of a quarter.

On the north side of the room, a window was shared with the bathroom. Evidently, the half bath had been put in as an afterthought.

You really couldn't see into the bathroom during the daytime, but later, we found out that if the lights were on in both rooms, the reflection of each could be seen in the other room's shared window. There wasn't a shower in the bath, so undressing wasn't a problem, but bathroom sounds and bedroom sounds could be plainly heard from one room to the other. So much for privacy!

Dan inspected the wall. "Oh, this wall is hokey. It's been put in just as a divider."

We went back downstairs and out the double Dutch door on the east side of the house. The wind slammed the door behind us.

Alice warned, "The door locks if it blows shut like that. I'll have my kids open it for us if we come back this way."

Dan held my hand as we walked across the porch. It was only a skeleton and really unsafe. The two-by-sixes holding up the rotten plywood were also loaded with dry rot.

"We'll have to replace this porch right off," he said.

After we stepped off, we could see the porch was rotten to the supports. Underneath it, a soccer ball sat among empty plastic cups, pop cans, broken toys, and cruddy garbage.

"Where's the septic system?" Dan asked.

"I think it's in that sunken area," Alice answered, pointing to a spot where the grass was somewhat greener.

He examined the ground but couldn't tell much. I followed him around to the north side of the house, where he crawled under.

"Hey, the piping is solid plastic—that's good. But there's no insulation—that's bad," he called back. After he crawled back out, he checked over the walls and the gutters. "Looks like cedar siding, but the gutters are in poor condition."

"We're interested," Dan told Alice as we said goodbye and got in the pickup.

Alice said, "The owner lives at the other number in the ad. Call her afternoon or evenings."

Dan started the engine. "I like it. What do you think?" he asked me.

"I like it too, but there's a lot of work to get done. If this is really something you want, I'll work hard at it with you," I promised.

He reached over and took my hand. "We're willing to do the work—all right then," he agreed. "But there's a lot of stuff that needs to be done that we don't know how to do. Of course, my dad does construction, and he will help with all the main structures like the porch, the foundation, the windows, putting up the siding, knocking down the wall, and replacing flooring.

"He knows how to put in a well, cause we just did it last year at his place. And he knows septic systems because we redid ours about five years ago. The old one wasn't standard plastic. The metal had to be replaced.

"My folks added on to our house. It was real small when we moved there. My dad let me help with a roofing project he bid on and got when I was seventeen, so I know something about roofing. And I worked in a plumbing shop and was an apprentice—so I've had a year and a half of plumbing. I'm really pretty good."

Dan was smart. He was good at figuring out how to run the water lines and how to replace stuff—without leaks.

"Dad and I don't know about the electrical—but my friend, David, is an electrician. He's working on his journeyman license. He works at an electrical company.

"And my friend, Jake, and his dad have a dry walling business. That means he could help us with sheetrock—

patching holes, patterning and texturing, and, of course, anything to do with the appearance of the ceiling and walls. He's really good at that. Jake's my age, twenty-three. He's always worked for his dad summers and now full time since he's been out of school."

I added, "My dad has done all the work in our house. He's done the plumbing, electrical, and sheet rocking. He's not as good as Jake at texture, but he's put in insulation, new windows, and replaced the flooring and the bathtub. And he rebuilds furniture. He's done everything to the house but the roof.

"Our house looks tons better. My dad can really do anything. He's never done carpeting—but I'm sure he'd catch right on if he watched."

Dan offered, "If our dads are willing, it looks like we'd have lots of help. And it could be fun doing everything the way we want it."

"It'd be almost like building a new house, too," I said. "Except that we already have a good foundation, a roof over our heads, and a place to live so we're not just paying rent. That's important. And I'll bet living in it will make us work faster."

"Okay, then. Alice said the owner lives at the other number. We'll call as soon as we get home."

As soon as he parked the car, Dan almost ran into the house, grabbed the phone, and dialed the other number. "Hello, this is Dan Grant. We've just looked at your place, and we're interested in it."

"Good, I'll put you on our list," the voice answered.

"Oh, there are others?"

"Yes—five. One couple has committed to come and talk tomorrow."

"Well, if they don't want it, you'll call me? If I'm not home, my fiancée, Merielena, will answer."

"Ok. I'll write that down. How do you spell Merielena?"

Monday afternoon when I got home from work, my future mother-in-law said, "The lady you two talked to yesterday called. She left her name and number."

I knew Dan would be happy. He had been real down when he thought other people on the list would take the house. I had been disappointed a little, but I always try to have a positive attitude. Changes are sometimes for the best in the long run.

I called the number right back, and we discussed a meeting time. I told her it would have to be the next weekend, because Dan and I had such weird work schedules. He worked nights, and I worked days. She suggested just the two of us meet sooner, if possible, to talk about a serious commitment. She still had others on her list.

I answered, "That should be okay. I work in downtown Astoria, and it wouldn't be any trouble for me to come up. How about Wednesday?"

That sounded okay to Dan, too, when I told him about the call, so on Wednesday, in the early afternoon, the owner, Meg, dropped by work and asked for me.

I came out of the back room and said, "Oh, hi. I'm Merielena. You must be Meg."

She said, "Yes, Roger and I wondered if you'd like to have a turkey sandwich with us when you drop by later?"

"Thanks, I like turkey sandwiches. I could be there around seven."

"That's good. We'll be expecting you. Just drive up 8th and turn right on Harrington."

I had been nervous about meeting the owners by myself, but Meg seemed friendly, so I felt better.

About 7:15 a.m. the next morning, as I was getting up, Dan got home from his night shift.

I told him that I had agreed for both of us to meet the owners at 3:00 p.m. on Saturday. "They know we're really interested. We discussed financing, and they seem to be agreeable to most kinds. I think we have a good chance at getting the place."

"Saturday sounds good. Now, did you get the answers to the questions you were supposed to ask? Was everything in the ad correct?"

"She said it was."

The ad had read:

> GREAT VIEWS—4 bedroom family home, 1 and 1/2 baths, lg shop/garage, 1.7 acres, for sale by owner, $99,000 now— $130,000 after work completed.

"She also said there were a lot of improvements that had to be made before commercial financing could be possible. She especially wanted the house occupied as soon as the renters leave—so it wouldn't get trashed while it was empty. Actually—further trashed," I added, "considering the way that Alice is leaving it."

We both laughed at that.

"Meg told me that a new well was in but not yet piped to the house, and the house would probably need a real septic system before financing. There is a special kind of expensive sand if the area isn't large enough, she said.

"Also, we may have to enlarge the east bedroom windows for fire reasons, and a banister would be essential for the stairs. And, she asked that we immediately replace the smoke alarms if they aren't working."

Dan was concentrating on all I was saying. The look on his face was serious. He said, "Good, the sooner we move, the better. Dad's always on my case about something or other. He thinks I don't know a damned thing. I'll be glad to prove him wrong once we're under our own roof."

I nodded. "I guess you know that the day we move in, we have to have the doors replaced—especially the front door. It was so warped, it wouldn't even shut all the way. Alice said she never even tries to lock the doors— and I absolutely won't live anyplace where I can't lock the doors," I stated with determination.

Dan knew I meant it. He respected how I felt about privacy and security.

"Especially when I'll be there by myself most nights until you pass your tests and get that new job."

We came to terms with the owners to rent/lease and to receive back half our rent money for the first year, if we took up our option. Dan took the necessary courses, easily passed his tests, got the new job, which paid twenty-five percent more, and took all the overtime he could get. I worked two jobs.

We were constantly exhausted as we repaired the house in what little spare time we had. We took out a householder's loan, and with the help of our parents and friends, we completely remodeled the living room, including painting the ceiling and walls, rewiring where necessary, replacing the back tile to the stove with a better grade, installing an economical pellet stove on a handsome platform, and replacing the carpets—actually twice, as the first new carpet was defective.

After several months of icy weather, the Sears troubleshooter revived the furnace in the area I had thoroughly scrubbed and disinfected.

Dan's father substituted several secure doors with sturdy locks for the warped ones and rebuilt the entryway from the foundation up the day we moved in. He later built a protected outside entry. My father immediately installed sound and motion security lights.

Dan—with lots of help—removed the holly tree in the front that had sheltered the moss growing on the roof, as well as the dangerously leaning remainder of the maple tree in the back, removed two spare chimneys, and replaced half of the roof.

He also built a splendid dog house and run for Prince, who came to us the first year in our home as a small pup—but didn't stay that way.

I often cleaned or painted until 2:00 a.m. in the morning. Sometimes on my early morning shift—after only three hours sleep—I arrived at work by 7:00 a.m. after driving for forty-five minutes on ice and snow.

We did all this in the first eleven months then took up a firm contract with the sellers—filing the final papers at the courthouse on the last icy day of the year—despite an expensively beautiful wedding in July and a honeymoon trip to Lake Tahoe.

Before the 2nd of July, we had almost completely redone the dining room and kitchen, with Dan installing a new stove, dishwasher, and sink, and new faucets and counters. He junked the worthless trash compacter and took it to the dump, as well as a ton of other junk Alice and her husband had left in back of the house. They didn't have the grace to be embarrassed by the mess, and they did forfeit the extra month's rent they had been offered for showing the house, rather than doing the toting themselves.

I painted, stained, stenciled, and did battle with rat nests, an army of spiders, and twenty years' accumulation of grime. Nothing escaped my broom, mop, and disinfectant.

Dan found a bargain on cedar siding. He and his dad put it up, bringing the home full circle to the mellow appearance of twenty years before. The first renter, Barbara, an overachiever at eight months into her second pregnancy, had obliterated the original redwood siding with barn-red paint.

Dan said it finally looked like home. I was very pleased.

"I'll never forget the way
Granddad's face looked..."

Hammers and Nails

Caitlyn M. Schmidt

I stood content, breathing the summer air. The sawdusty scent of freshly cut wood mixed into the breeze, which whispered in the alder trees that adorned my backyard. Their leaves and trunks were smudges of ash and emerald painted in the backdrop of my vision.

I was three years old, and the sun's white glow was blindingly bright as I looked upwards at an old man with gentle eyes and straight, white hair. He had a lined forehead and crinkles in his cheeks.

My grandfather's rich and faintly gravelly voice floated in the air while he conversed with my father, who stood nearby. I heard the hint of honey in Daddy's deep voice but could not see his face—yet in my mind's eye, I knew his wavy, ash blonde hair, dark blue eyes, and groomed mustache well. He always smelled like shaving cream, ironed dress shirts, and his faithful leather briefcase.

Next to us rested a wooden playset. Its construction was in progress, but it was almost complete. It would have a tower with a white and blue striped canvas top, a ladder, a bright yellow slide, and two creaking swings suspended by crisp, white rope. Later, Daddy would add to my delight by appending a set of monkey bars with a rope ladder for access, as well as a swing glider. But at that time, I was more than happy with what he and Granddad were building for me.

Like the engineers they were, they had opted to

assemble the playset kit themselves. Though I, of course, took no part in the decision, I was inclined to stand with them and watch while they completed their task. I was curious; I wanted to know what they were doing. I wanted to see it happen.

This was the biggest present I had ever received, and perhaps the most impressive, especially to my young, wide eyes and constantly wandering mind. I was eager for the moment I'd be allowed to begin my exploration of this grand, new thing in my life. I wanted to venture to the top of the tower, glide down the glossy slide, and feel the wind as Daddy or Mommy pushed me in the dandelion-yellow swing.

I didn't realize it then, but the playset would become a cornerstone of my childhood fun and imaginary games. I didn't know it then, but it would remain in its spot until I was much too old to use it. I didn't understand it then, but it was a special gift built with something stronger than saws and hammers and nails and screws.

My grandfather would continue loving me for five more years before he was gone and began to love me from somewhere intangible. But I didn't know it then— the moment was void of worry. It did not contain darkness or sorrow; I, blue-eyed and filled with wonder, could not fathom such things.

It's a memory brimming with light and love and dreams for the future. I'll never forget the way Granddad's face looked in that white sunlight as I gazed up at him, filled with a tranquil joy that emanated from the simple act of father and son building with hammers and nails.

****

Granddad had long ago put up a fence to protect Grandma's treasured rose garden, which was nestled between the gravel access road and their home's atrium. It also served the purpose of creating a defined backyard on their large Eugene, Oregon property. When I was seven years old, I was allowed to be outside alone during summer visits to the farm—as long as I stayed within the boundaries of his brown picket fence.

Ignoring the moss between the crumbling flagstone paving, I danced to my own melody, my long hair twisting as I twirled, playing the part of a princess wandering her castle grounds. Being an only child, I had become quite good at entertaining myself.

In trilling mumbles, I spoke of my loneliness and longing. I was waiting for Prince Charming to find me and take me on a magical quest to explore the corners of my kingdom. My land was a vast twenty acres, complete with royal stables, royal woods, and a royal river marking the realm's edge.

I inspected the pink, ivory, and red flowers of my royal rose bed. Their delicate candied aroma whirled in the sun-soaked breeze. As I pretended to prick my finger on an olive green thorn, I heard a rustle in the grass that didn't belong to the wind. I looked up.

A fawn, its tawny fur adorned with snow-white spots, had emerged from the forest. It began to munch on the grass sprouting below a small grove of apple trees less than twenty feet away.

Slowly, I moved closer, unlatched the gate of Granddad's fence, and began to cross the gravel road that separated the house and garden from the forest's edge. With a small click, the gate swung shut behind me.

Dust awoken by my footsteps settled as I reached the border of the grassy terrain. A giggle escaped me, and the baby deer's bowed head snapped up, its black nose pointing straight at my smiling face.

The curiosity in its round eyes matched my own. I stepped forward cautiously. It tilted its head. Blackberry bushes and rhododendrons towered to my right, and the apple trees were scattered to my left. The fawn was frozen between them, its oversized ears aimed in my direction. We were trapped in a doe-eyed stare.

It was a moment of discovery, of adventure. Why

was exploring unaccompanied beyond the rose garden's perimeter a forbidden activity? I, the lonely, confined princess, had yearned for this! But soon, I would yearn for the protection of Granddad's old fence.

From behind the rhododendrons strode a proud figure. A father stood, his crown of branching bone prepared to protect his child from the human invading their territory. The buck's breath whooshed from his nostrils.

I dared not move. Picturing the beast charging toward me, its antlers aimed at a princess in peril, I held my breath. Then, the cage surrounding me in that moment was shattered by the smooth sound of a sliding glass door being opened. I whipped my head around in response to see who'd emerged from inside the atrium.

My father stood, prepared to protect his child from the large buck endangering his daughter's safety. Daddy quietly passed through Grandma's rose garden and asked me to walk backwards.

"Slowly," he instructed.

The gravel crackled as my feet traveled in reverse.

Daddy opened Granddad's gate and then his arms, and I found his hands comforting as he lifted me up. He held me tightly, my soft face resting against his scratchy but familiar five o'clock shadow, and I knew I was out of harm's reach.

The buck bolted, and the fawn followed close behind. My father released a coffee-scented sigh of relief and carried me inside.

Caitlyn M. Schmidt was born and raised in the Seattle, Washington area. She graduated with a degree in English with an Emphasis on Creative Writing from Western Washington University. Caitlyn has already visited six continents and loves experiencing new cultures and historic sites. She was married in 2016 and currently works in Seattle.

"And do you know who has the biggest standing army in the world today?"

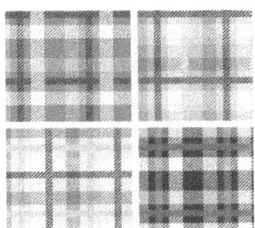

Upholstery Man

Anonymous

I needed to have some upholstery work done, so I went to a local shop to inquire about the job and pick up some fabric samples to take home with me. That's where I met Cab. While I looked through the sample books, we visited.

"Never did very good in school," he told me. "Too busy causing trouble. But I got a good business now.

"When I was in fifth grade, there was this girl with a speech problem. Hardly never said anything anyone could understand. Hardly never said anything at all. Didn't pay any attention to the teacher either. She read all the time, and once when the teacher gave a hard test, that girl handed it in, in less than five minutes.

"The teacher yelled at her—figured she'd cheated. So she gave the girl another test, a harder one. She finished that one in less time, yet got 100 percent. The teacher said, 'That's incredible!'

"That girl was brilliant. Teacher flunked all the rest of us that year. She was always beating on us too—we were so ornery. That girl often let me know when Teacher was gonna get me. I got hit the most," Cab said, quite proudly. "But, would you believe that teacher brought me new shirts and shoes that year, and a tie for the Christmas pageant?"

"Despite how bad you were, she must have liked you anyway," I noted.

"Yeah, she liked me. I was so bad, she couldn't help

but notice me. But sometimes, it's the bad ones that have the personality," he explained, his wiry frame expanding a little past my height.

"Yes, I know. I was a teacher, and I had bad ones, too, I couldn't help but like."

"You was a teacher? You know, that fifth grade teacher, Mrs. Grumman, moved away, but she was always asking about me, and when I went into the Army—the National Guard—and was home on leave before I left for the Korean Conflict, she sent word she wanted to see me. "

"Did you go?"

"Yeah, I went."

"Was she glad to see you?"

"You bet she was."

"Whatever happened to the girl—the one who hardly spoke?" I asked.

"Last I heard, she was a professor in some big university."

"That's good, but I hope she had speech therapy somewhere first."

"Yeah, I hope she did, too. She was really smart. I didn't learn much in school. But I did learn to work. At fifteen, I went to work after school and on weekends in a furniture factory. At first, I swept out and cleaned up, but it wasn't long till I learned the trade. And I could turn out thirteen set-ups a day."

"Thirteen? From the ground up?"

"Nah. Others did the wood and the springs. The covers were plain. I put in the padding, and you just tack it down on all four sides and then put a tack about every three-fourths inch. It'll hold. Some would put tacks each by each. But that ain't necessary—a waste of time. Mine always lasted fine."

"Where was this?" I inquired.

"Wilkesburg, Pennsylvania," Cab responded.

"Coal mining country?"

"Yeah, all the people were hard working, first generation Americans from European countries:

Germans, Poles, Irish, Hungarians—lotsa Hungarians—always Italians, Spanish, some Portuguese—all good hard-working people."

"Where was your family from?"

"Spain."

"Really?"

I would have guessed Italy from the way he spoke, but then I looked at him closely. The silvery stubble on his head was almost as closely shaven as his face, which wasn't very. But, his ears and other features reminded me of the Basque. I didn't say Basque, however, in case he wasn't. The Basques and the Spanish, of course, being like the Indians and the Pakistanis.

"Sure, back in those days, you could trust any bargain with a handshake. Nowadays, you can't trust nobody. But I met a lot of good people in the war."

"My husband was in the Chosin Reservoir Battle. Were you there?"

"Yes, I was there—and a quarter million Chinese, too. And do you know who has the biggest standing army in the world today? It ain't the USA."

"And not the Russians," I added.

"Nope, not the Russians—it's the Chinese," Cab told me.

"That's interesting, especially because Chinese families are only allowed one child now, and most of those single children are boys. It won't be long—in fact, it's already begun—before those single young men can't find wives. Then, China will have all those extra young men, with all that testosterone, in a very frustrating situation. Do you know what the old Irish Kings used to do?" I asked him.

"What did they do?"

This was a man who obviously enjoyed history. He had become the avid student he never was in fifth grade. If she could only see him now, Mrs. Grumman would be very proud.

"Well," I continued, "when old Ireland would become too peaceful and too prolific for its small area, the kings of the different clans would get together and declare war so it would kill off the extra male population."

"Wow!" Cab exclaimed. "Now that's something to think about—with all those extra Chinese and a few atomic bombs, they could raise quite a stink."

Cab opened the door for me.

"I'll bring these samples back in a couple days, if that's all right," I said.

"No hurry. Nice talkin' to you. I'll have to get me a book on China."

He left the door open and looked through the screen until my engine started. Cab waved as I pulled away, my headlights shining into the mist.

"I heard a woman's voice say, 'I have a gun. Give me all your money!'"

Shoot-Out at McDonald's, Sort Of

Kami Allen

A number of years ago, my then five-year-old daughter, Amaya, and I, had been to a barbeque one evening. Since we're vegans, we'd only eaten potato chips, and I was starving when we left the gathering.

I pulled into a McDonald's to order a salad, and the drive-thru window order box asked, "How can I help you?"

I answered, "Just a minute," as I turned around to see if Amaya was awake, and if she wanted anything to eat. She was sound asleep.

When I turned back around, an arm came through my car window, which fortunately, I'd opened only about four inches. Then, I heard a woman's voice say, "I have a gun. Give me all your money!" and saw a ski mask covering the face at the other end of the arm.

Looking at the outstretched hand in my car and the ski masked face in the dark—it was 1:30 a.m. in the morning—I instinctively pushed the automatic "up" button, which trapped her arm in the window. At the same time, my right hand slammed down on the horn. I held onto the window button as the motor kept winding, trying to close it, pressing up on her arm, and kept my other hand on the horn, which kept blaring loudly.

The woman started swinging her arm, trying to hit

me in the face while yelling, "Let go of my arm!" and repeating, "I have a gun! Give me all your money!"

I yelled back at her, "No! I'm not letting go. You put your arm in my car. It's mine now!" as I kept pressing the button, keeping her arm firmly imprisoned.

Then, Amaya woke up and saw what was happening. She was scared to death and started crying and screaming.

The woman continued swinging at me, hoping to hit me so I would release her. Instead, I bit down hard on her bare arm, and she let out a bloodcurdling scream. I let go, as I didn't care to bite her down to the bone.

She ripped off her ski mask and wailed, "Please, let me go. I have a little boy at home!"

I hollered, "I don't care! My little girl is here with me. You scared her to death! You put your arm in my car, and I'm not letting you go."

She started crying frantically. The window was pressing on the main artery in her arm, and she was in pain. She was getting weak, and her body began to sag, but her arm, still tightly caught in my car window, was holding her up.

We were making quite a scene—the thwarted thief was screaming, I was yelling and honking the horn, and my little girl was hysterically screaming and crying.

Finally, one of the McDonald's employees—having heard all the commotion through the order box—came outside to see exactly what was going on. In my rearview mirror, I could see him just standing and watching us. It felt like forever before he eventually went back inside, hopefully to call 911.

Time seemed to stand still while all the screaming, yelling, crying, and honking continued.

At last, two sheriff's deputies and three police officers arrived and surrounded my car. I didn't stop honking or release the woman's arm from the window until the first policeman reached the bumper of my car.

The officer grabbed her as she was sliding to the ground, and her jacket zipper scratched my car door.

Several more officers ran up and assisted the first in taking the woman to a police car.

She had quickly revived, and she began kicking, screaming, and shouting, "Let me go! I haven't done anything wrong! She tried to kill me!"

A police officer came to my car door just as I was trying to get out and check on Amaya.

He said, "Just sit down, miss, and try to relax. I need to get some information from you."

I cried out, "No!" and pushed him aside and got out of the car. "My five-year-old daughter is in the back seat. I need to get to her, now!"

He exclaimed, "Oh my God! You have a child with you?"

We both hurried around to the other side of the car to get to Amaya. He pulled the door open, and I pulled my little girl into my arms and held her tightly. I tried to soothe her and calm her down while I answered the officer's questions.

When we finally made it home and into bed, I held Amaya for the rest of the night. She had frightening nightmares for over a month after the incident. Mine lasted for over two months.

I found out later that the woman who tried to rob me was named Sarah. I actually knew her, as we'd both gone to the same high school. She was a few grades behind me, and I had not known her well, and hadn't wanted to, as she was always getting into trouble.

Sarah had three court hearings after her arrest. In the last one, she was sentenced to prison for fifteen years for the attempted robbery. She had the possibility for release in two years for good behavior but would be on parole for five years. Sarah already had a record and had been in and out of jail previously, several times, on drug-related charges.

The same night she stuck her arm in my car window, she had tried to rob the McDonald's. They'd scoffed at her and shoved her out the door but hadn't called the police. She was still hanging around the parking lot when I drove up, and she evidently thought a lone woman would be easy pickings.

Earlier that same evening, she'd been seen stealing prescription medications from purses in several different bars around town. She lied to me about having a little boy at home—he had been taken from her by the Department of Human Services and put into foster care.

If I had been in the mood to give her clemency—which I was not—I could have blamed Sarah's bad actions on her mother, who'd done drugs and alcohol throughout her daughter's life—even sharing tokes and drinks with Sarah during early adolescence.

When Sarah failed to appear at one of her hearings, a warrant was put out for her arrest. When they found her, she tested positive for drugs and was sent back to prison for twelve years, with no chance of early parole.

And to top it all off, I never did get my salad from McDonald's that night.

Kami Allen is multi-talented. She draws and writes with ease. She was working as a guard at the Astoria Aquatic Center when the above incident occurred.

"'Her office is only a few blocks away—
she can see the World Trade Center.'"

9/11/2001
Oregon Coast

Eckley Guerin

The phone rang over a dozen times. This was before we got an answering machine.

"Must be one of the kids," I mumbled. "No one's that persistent, except one of them. I wonder what's gone wrong now."

I went barefoot to the phone in the other upstairs bedroom and picked it up. "Yes, dear, what's wrong?"

"Mom, don't worry. She's all right."

"What do you mean? Who's all right?"

"Sis is all right. She didn't go to work today."

"No, she was planning to take a flight out here to Oregon this afternoon. Why shouldn't she be all right?"

"Then you haven't heard about New York City being bombed?"

"Oh no! The whole city?"

"No, the north and south towers of the World Trade Center. They just went down. Turn on your TV."

"I'll go downstairs. But how do you know she's all right?"

"Loren called. He called her at work as soon as he heard about the planes. They said she had the week off, so he called her home phone. She was there, and she's all right."

"Her office is only a few blocks away—she can see the World Trade Center from a window on her floor. But her apartment is at the northern end of the island. I'll go down now and turn on the TV. Thanks for calling me, Benj."

"You're welcome. I told Loren I'd call you. He's at work."

Downstairs, the TV screen showed a beautiful blue sky over downtown New York City, with a plane hitting a tower in front of gorgeous white clouds. Then flames spewed from an explosion, and a plane hit a second tower. Another explosion, more flames. One tower went down, then the other.

This was shown over and over and over again.

It was September 11, 2001, where in the Northwest, the Southwest, the Southeast, the Midwest, the New England States, and all over the rest of the world, we watched our TVs in horror! We looked on helplessly at what was happening in New York City, Washington, D.C., and the Pennsylvania countryside, where a heroic band of passengers brought down the third airplane taken over by terrorists.

It was a day of unfathomable loss for our entire country, and for the world.

"...'the blackout's affected at least 15,000,000 people.'"

The Most Extensive Blackout in the USA
New York City, August 14, 2003

Emma von Hoven

"Mom, do you know all of New York City is out of power?"

"Yes, Bonnie, I do. We've been worried. Are you okay?"

"I'm fine. What do you know? We have no power at all—no TV, no news. We don't know even if it's terrorists!"

"I heard it wasn't terrorists. We haven't listened to the news yet. Dad is watching a shoot-em-up movie. All I know is what I overheard a lady say in a store downtown. She said it evidently isn't terrorists, but most of the East Coast and Midwest don't have power, and that's all she said—so that's all I know."

"How long ago was that?"

"This afternoon. Maybe half an hour ago—about 4:45 p.m. our time. She said she thought it went out about 4:10 p.m. Pacific Time. I'm so glad to hear your voice. You didn't answer your phone, so I was afraid you might be stuck somewhere."

"No, I'm okay. I'm at Matt's place. We're sitting out on the balcony. Mom, could you listen to the news for me and call me back with what you hear? I don't have my cell phone with me. Here's Matt's number."

"Sure, Bonnie, I'll turn the radio on now and call you

147

back in half an hour or less."

Twenty-five minutes later, Matt's phone rang.

"Bonnie?"

"Yes, Mom. What did you find out?"

"All the electricity's out, west to Detroit and north to Ottawa. Detroit, Lansing, and Ann Arbor—all out. Much or all of New York state and New Jersey, and from Toledo to Cleveland. Planes that are circling or ready to land can come into the almost blacked out airfields— LaGuardia, Kennedy, and Islip. They have generators, but no planes can leave. All subways and trains in and out of New York City are shut down. The last New York outage was in 1999."

"I remember, Mom. I was already living here, but we didn't worry about terrorists back then. Anything else?"

"Con Edison Headquarters is dark. Everyone's using flashlights there. Do you have flashlights or candles?"

"Matt has two candles, but we haven't used them yet."

"Daddy says to be very careful with them if you do. You know how dangerous candles can be."

"I know. Fire trucks have already been making runs. I can hear a siren now."

"I'll listen to some more news and call you back."

"Thanks, Mom. You're our only source of info. No one else knows anything here. It's even hard to get out on cell phones."

A few hours later, Matt's phone rang again.

"Hi, Bonnie. Everything okay?"

"Yes, we're fine. It's plenty warm—but there's a breeze. We're just sitting here watching car lights. They're going really slow. There are no traffic lights."

"Can you see the stars? Mars is the closest it's been in sixty million years. The moon is to our south at about 11:00 p.m. Pacific Time, and Mars just to the left."

"It is? We'll look for it. The moon is big, and, yes, we're on the tenth floor, so we can see the stars. Really unusual because the shine of the city lights usually blocks the glow of the stars. On a really clear night, we can usually only see maybe ten bright stars and a few planets. Nice to see so many tonight. Now, what did you find out?"

"Well, the blackout's affected at least 15,000,000 people. Six hundred railway and subway cars were running at the time of the blackout. Thirty-three full railway trains were halted. They don't know how many people were caught in elevators. One man said his elevator was stuck between floors. He hollered and banged. Someone heard him and said to wait a few minutes. Eventually, they pried open the doors, and he threw out his bag and then climbed up and out."

"I imagine a lot of people were stuck in elevators. I'm just glad I wasn't on a subway. I hate the thought of having to walk out in the dark with all those rats and who knows what else scuttling around."

"Yes, they have been bringing people out of stalled cars, sometimes up ladders four stories tall, or through dark tunnels with puddles of stagnant water, and rats, and what have you."

"Yuck!"

"Sweetheart, Mary and I are going out for a long walk. It's after seven now. I'll watch the nine o'clock news and then call you. Oh, will you be up? It'll be after midnight Eastern Time."

"Yes, I'll stay up, Mom. I really want to know what's going on."

Shortly after 12:30 a.m., Bonnie heard the phone and picked up. "Hi, Mom."

"Hi, Bonnie, the Niagara Falls power is working fine. It wasn't the cause. The problem is the transmission grid has to be balanced. They haven't built transmission lines in many years. We use so much electricity—we have overloads. The system is vulnerable to this kind of overload. It could happen again. We need to build intrastate transmission lines. Green tea blocks cancer nodes in bladder."

"Mom, you just made that up."

"No, I didn't. I'm reading CNN's TV crawler, and

that's what it said. Also, a man fell down between the subway tracks. He flattened out, and the train passed over him. He's injured but should live."

"We heard that earlier—before the power went off."

"Wolf Blitzer is on the street in Lower Manhattan. He says there are only lights from private energy generators. But parts of Westchester County are on. Also Long Island and Hoboken—must have their own generators. Cars and buses are moving, but there are no traffic lights or streetlights. Hundreds and thousands of people walked home. Some walked for five hours. Evidently, two bridges lead across the river. One is the Brooklyn. TV showed a flash of one bridge lightly packed, but the other bridge scene showed it was totally jammed."

"The other bridge must be the George Washington. It leads over to New Jersey."

"One announcement said the power in New York City should all be on by one—another contradicted that. Mary said she saw on her TV where a fifty-two-year-old woman was out directing traffic. She'd just had a back operation but was doing a good job. I can't believe it was a recent operation."

"Maybe she just had a mole removed. But it is encouraging that Long Island, Hoboken, and part of Westchester is on. Perhaps it won't be too much longer for us."

"I hope not. Over 600 subway and commuter cars were stalled. All but six have been evacuated. Forty thousand police and firemen are to be deployed in the city overnight. The Coast Guard may be delivering water. Twenty-one power plants shut down in just three minutes. Three of them were nuclear."

"Imagine being stuck in a subway car for almost six hours. It must be awful—especially if you have claustrophobia."

"I think it was your mayor who said when the power does come on, to economize. Don't run your air conditioner or all your other appliances."

"We'll be thrifty. Thanks so much, Mom, for all your news. We wouldn't have the faintest idea otherwise. Will you call again tomorrow, if we're still off?"

"Yes, I will. You know how late I read at night. But I'll call as early as I can."

It was almost noon when the phone rang in NYC.

"Hi, Bonnie. Dad says you have lights."

"Yes, thank goodness. We've had them since about six this morning. I was just waking up when I thought I heard music, and sure enough, it was coming from the SciFi channel. But, because we had a cable glitch yesterday before all the power went out, our channel changer isn't working, so I can't turn it to news and find out anything.

"Matt's roommate, Luke, was at work, and after his shift, he worked another to pay back a friend. He's going to be stuck working two more security shifts anyway. At least he'll get overtime, and he can use it. The restaurant in his building remembered he was there and brought him some food, and one of the staff stayed long enough for him to go out and make a phone call to us. His cell phone wasn't working from where he was in the basement. We were glad to hear from him. We were beginning to worry."

"That's good. I don't know much more, except they think it started around Lake Erie. It seems to have been a domino effect. According to Bill Richardson, Clinton's energy secretary, and now the governor of New Mexico, we're a major superpower with a Third World power transmission system. Our grid is antiquated and needs serious modernization—which will amount to billions and billions. I guess Bush's trillion-dollar tax cuts could have covered it."

"Sure leaves us vulnerable. I'll bet the terrorists are glad to hear all that. We're really surprised they weren't the cause of this one. Say, Mom, what about the stuff in our fridge? We got it yesterday morning, and we only opened the door twice—once to grab out a block of cheese, and once to get some drinks. Should the food be all right? All the meat was in the freezer part, and there's still some ice left in the water in the freezer trays. Electricity was off about fourteen hours."

"If it smells all right, it should be ok. If anything smells funny, dump it. If there's still ice in the trays, and it was only fourteen hours, it should be all right. How's your friend, Anna? Is she ok?"

"I thought I told you she's been so sick—she was in the emergency room three or four times last month. She doesn't have any health benefits, and even though she had a temp job, they were pretty mean about her being unavailable so often, so she just gave up. She needs an operation, really. She and her roommate sold what they could, gave a lot away, packed up, and took a Greyhound to California last week."

"That's too bad. She was the one who got you that good job when you first got to New York, wasn't she?"

"Yes, with Power Productions. That was a great job, terrific benefits and perks. They even served free lunch—and a lot of fun. Too bad they closed their New York office. Though, with their recommendations, I got the job at MTV."

"How's the job situation, now?"

"Terrible, Mom. I try for everything I'm the least bit qualified for. But last week's possibility had 220 resumes turned in. They're supposed to read them all, but I'll bet they won't. I don't know what I'd do without you two to fall back on. Lots of people are having to let their apartments go and move back to where they came from. A lot of people are living on the streets. It's really awful."

"I know, dear. And we worry about you not having any health insurance."

"Me too. I had a dreadful cold last week, but I was able to go to rehearsal. I just sang through it."

"You sound pretty good now. Well, I guess we're not supposed to tie up the lines, so I'll hang up. Glad you're fine. Bye for now. Love you."

"Bye, Mom, thanks. Love you, too."

✴✴✴✴✴✴✴✴✴✴✴✴✴✴✴✴

The economy in NYC was still trying to recover from the 9/11/2001 attacks. Fifteen million hook-ups were out of power during the blackout. More than $6,000,000,000 was the estimated cost to get the nation back up to speed from those fourteen hours.

After a three-month investigation, much of the blame was laid on First Energy in Ohio, where a non-working control room alarm left operators unaware that three high-voltage lines had gone out of service after contact with trees. Other power companies suffered from outdated equipment.

Before 9/11/2001, Emma von Hoven's daughter, Bonnie, had an excellent job as an executive assistant on the fifty-first floor in the MTV Tower in New York City, and she could see the Twin Towers from her office.

The 9/11 tragedy was devastating to those personally involved, and to the entire country. The ensuing downfall of the NYC economy, and the resulting massive layoffs, erased her daughter's job, and she ended up being one of the 100,000 jobless in Lower Manhattan.

"Ghosts can be mischievous..."

The Veil Is Thin

Gail Starr

It was the evening of the summer solstice. My roommate, Andrew, a computer and music geek, was taking a shower before going out to help a friend with his late-night program on KMUN, our community radio station in Astoria, Oregon.

The geek—though he's much too handsome to be called a geek—noticed doors in the house were opening and shutting, opening and shutting—but he heard no footsteps, no creaks. The house is almost a hundred years old, and it *always* creaks in warm weather.

At first, Andrew thought I'd come home. But I keep bells on my bedroom door, and there weren't any bells jingling. So, it had to be other doors.

When he got out of the shower, he checked all the upstairs doors. None of them were in different positions from when he'd last walked down the hall. Nothing was changed. No one else was home.

I came home from my solstice party about 11:15 p.m. Andrew had been and gone and was back, and he told me about hearing doors banging.

So I said, "The fact is, Andrew, the veil is thin. The ghosts have gotten to know you and no longer practice quietude. They just go about their normal business. I hope you'll consider that a compliment.

"I've had very long talks with the ghosts. They are really quite agreeable. They do what they're told. I've informed them firmly, 'You can't be scaring off my roommates. It's because of them I am able to keep a roof over your heads—and mine. An almost one-hundred-year-old house needs a lot of fixing up. And please don't forget it.'"

About twelve years ago when my husband and I first moved in, and before we had any boarders, we slept in the east room.

One night, just after we'd gone to bed, I exclaimed, "Jerry, there is somebody walking down the hall!"

He answered, "Oh, you know these old houses—they creak all the time."

It happened that a full moon was rising that night, and the sound of the tread was measured. Footfall, creak... footfall, creak... footfall, creak...

"Don't tell me it's just a noisy old house!"

Then the footsteps stopped. My husband fell right to sleep. I didn't.

Around the time of the Gulf War, about 1992, it was a stormy night—a howling, blowing southwester in full force when I went to bed. I fell fast asleep. Much later, in the middle of the night, the storm continued to howl outside. I was in the north room, which overlooks the Columbia River. The blinds were shut tight.

All of a sudden, I opened my eyes to see a light in my bedroom. Still nearly asleep, I reached up to turn the light off—but I actually turned it on. So, I really turned it off and went back to sleep.

The storm continued to blow, and the rain continued to pelt the windows. Sound asleep with my eyes closed tight, the room lit up again to the brightness of about a twenty-watt bulb.

I keep a sixty-watt bulb in my lamp so I can read. This was definitely dimmer, but certainly not darkness. I turned it off.

These ridiculous maneuvers happened twice more. Annoyed, I pronounced, "Okay, you guys. Just cool it! I've got to go to work tomorrow."

I snapped off the light one final time. It stayed off for the rest of the night. Ghosts can be mischievous, but they know when enough is enough.

I rented a room to Enke about two years later. She was reading in the east room when the doorknob began to turn. She thought someone wanted to come in. She leaned over and pulled the door open. Nobody was there.

She came down to the kitchen where three of us were talking. We women always hung out in the kitchen—that's where the food was.

Enke asked, "Did anyone want to speak to me? The doorknob was twisting on the door, but no one was there."

I explained, "It was just a ghost."

I really don't know if there is one ghost or more. Maybe it's just one, and he has visitors. But, since the house turned one hundred years old in 2005, it's no surprise we have ghosts.

I talk to them a lot. They are good about minding—but they never talk aloud—except for that Saturday evening on the summer solstice, with awesome Andrew's banging doors.

As I showered about midnight that night, I heard music—strange half notes. Eerie!

Gail Starr teaches at Tongue Point Learning Center, makes art prints, draws, sculpts, and also works with elderly patients in their homes. She knows many fascinating stories.

"We watched with a sick fascination as the hurricane developed and came closer and closer."

Surviving Charles, Frances, and Ivan

Pat Williams

When I left northwest Oregon for Pensacola, Florida, on August 15, 2004, I thought my biggest adventure—other than seeing the family and meeting my new grandchild—would be my cross-country Greyhound bus trip. That trip was an adventure, all right, but it took a backseat to hurricanes Charles, Frances, and Ivan.

I'll admit, I thought it would be exciting to be in hurricane country, and shortly after I arrived, Charles went through Florida. The threat was especially scary at first, because we weren't sure where it was going to make landfall.

I was visiting my pregnant daughter, Shani, her husband, Tim, and my two-and-a-half-year-old grandson, Jason. We relaxed somewhat when we realized it wasn't coming our way or planning to hit the Palm Coast where Tim's cousins, the Unverzagts, lived. Charles crossed Florida on a diagonal from west to east and did lots of damage where it did hit, though.

Right on the heels of Charlie came Frances. Once more, we held our breath and kept vigil in front of the television as events unfolded. We watched with a sick fascination as the hurricane developed and came closer and closer.

When its path became definite, we realized it was heading for the St. Augustine area where Tim's cousins lived. Frantic calls back and forth arranged for them to come to Pensacola to stay with us.

They secured their home, loaded up the pets and whatever else would fit in their two vehicles, and headed across the state. After the four of them arrived Thursday around noon, all of us sat mesmerized, watching the television hurricane news.

The Unverzagts had looked for, but hadn't found, a generator in their area. So, Tim helped them search the Pensacola area that afternoon, and they felt really lucky when they finally found one at a decent price. The rest of us hadn't paid much attention to their search or even their elation at having found one. It hadn't occurred to Tim, Shani, or me how terribly important and necessary this piece of equipment was for even meager living under hurricane conditions.

We all thought it was neat and were interested enough to go to the garage to admire the new beast, but, beyond that, we didn't really think about it much. However, after we heard how much use some of their neighbors had made of theirs in St. Augustine, and fearing what difficult conditions we might face in Pensacola throughout hurricane season, all of us fell seriously in love with generators.

While the Unverzagt cousins were with us in Pensacola, their only contact with home was via the television and cell phone calls to neighbors and friends. Finally, on Tuesday, September 7, after Hurricane Frances had moved away from their area, it was time for them to head home to check out how bad things really were.

They called to tell us when they arrived. Although there was quite a bit of damage in their neighborhood, their house was okay, and they had lost only one tree. We thought it was safe to relax. Little did we know what was right around the corner, lurking in the Caribbean.

Since I'd arrived in Pensacola, we'd been joking

about when Shani would have the baby. Tim told Shani that she should wait until September because he really liked the September birthstone, sapphire, better than her August birthstone, peridot.

Unfortunately, when Tim came home from work on Tuesday, September 7, his mood was serious, and he told Shani, "It's time to have the baby before this weekend. There's another hurricane forming."

Suddenly, it didn't seem very funny to any of us. On Friday, September 7, Shani learned that if Hurricane Ivan threatened between then and her delivery date, she was supposed to check into the hospital, which was also an evacuation shelter. But the rest of the family would need to find another shelter. The idea of splitting up the family during a hurricane made us all nervous.

As a result, Shani and the baby listened when Tim said it was time to get the job done. Early the next morning, Wednesday, September 8, Shani went into labor. Tim took her to the hospital about 4:00 a.m., and Alex was born that day at 8:02 a.m.

On Friday, September 10, Shani and Alex came home. Although we were glad to have them there, we were practically glued to the television watching what was happening with Ivan. Every newscast showed it getting closer and closer to us. By Sunday, September 12, we were really concerned. There were no more hurricane jokes. Suddenly, it became very real.

As the weekend progressed, it was increasingly obvious the hurricane wasn't going to cooperate and go away. It was so scary and nerve-wracking to sit and watch the television weather forecaster point at his map—right where we were located—and say, "This is where it's going to hit."

Late Sunday morning, Tim and three neighbors went looking for plywood—a new experience for each of them. They didn't realize just how quickly plywood would become precious, therefore very difficult to find. After hours of searching, they returned with enough plywood and screws to cover the windows and doors of all four homes and immediately started putting it up. By the time the last of the four houses was boarded up, it was after midnight.

Although Shani and I got some things sorted and packed on Sunday, it wasn't until Monday that it fully hit us—we had to leave! So, we shifted into high gear. We tried to continue functioning as usual, but with plywood covering all the windows, and tape crisscrossing the insides of them, it felt like we were in the Twilight Zone.

One thing you don't think of until a time like this is—what do we do with the pets? Luckily, we didn't have dogs or cats to consider, but Shani's fish—a beta named Fireball—had to be left behind. We thought he had a better chance at home than being taken, splashing in a bowl, across the state.

We put the fish bowl in the small bathroom in the center of the house and hoped for the best. Of course, as the family's time away from him stretched out, the probability Fireball wouldn't make it became more of a possibility. It was hard to deal with.

As things began to look more serious, we made calls to the Unverzagts on Florida's east coast to make arrangements for us to go there. Tim wanted us to head out of the area early Tuesday, but there was still a lot to do. He was trying to get pictures of everything inside of the house for insurance purposes. Shani worked as hard as possible, and I needed direction with everything I did.

Little Jason was perplexed by everything—the addition of a grandma to the household, a new baby who demanded his mother's time and energy, and now all the commotion about the hurricane. As a result, he needed a lot of extra tender loving care, which was proving difficult because we adults were getting more and more nervous and stressed.

Since Tim was in the Navy, he had pre-arranged for two weeks leave to help with the baby. So, he was basically off duty. We just had to pack, get the house secured, and leave.

Other families on the street weren't so lucky. Two of the men—also in the Navy—had signed up for duty at evacuation centers and were to be responsible for students from their classes at the naval base. Because of this, both of their families would be going to the evacuation centers with them, instead of leaving the area.

At least one family on the street had apparently decided to ride out the storm in their home. The day we left, we drove down the street waving and saying our goodbyes to the neighbors. It was really hard to get in the car and drive off not knowing how they would come through the storm.

I don't really think any of us completely understood what might happen. All of the adults were fragmented and frazzled. The kids—from Jason's age to teenagers—were confused, excited, and scared.

Heading out of Pensacola, we didn't notice any difference in the traffic, people's activities, or the weather. Further out of town, the traffic got thicker and slower.

We hadn't been on the road very long when we saw the first caravan of utility company trucks headed toward Pensacola. By the time we got to Tallahassee, we had counted between twelve and fifteen groups, some of them with as many as ten to twenty trucks.

Seeing all those workers leaving the area where Hurricane Frances had just hit, and going to where Ivan was predicted to make landfall, made me want to cry. How long had those people been away from their own families? How long would it be before they could go home? Would they go home to damage and destruction?

We knew we had a long drive ahead of us. The Unverzagts' home was in the community of Palm Coast, a few miles south of St. Augustine. This trip was comparable to driving from Astoria, on the northwest Oregon coast, to Ashland, in southwest Oregon, not far from the California border.

We figured it would take us about eight hours. The

traffic was stop-and-go much of the time, and thirty-five to forty miles per hour was our speed. Every rest stop was filled to overflowing with people getting away from the hurricane, or emergency crews heading into the hurricane area.

We left Pensacola at 2:45 p.m. on Tuesday. It was almost 5:00 a.m. on Wednesday morning when we arrived in Palm Coast, after almost fifteen hours on the road—but we had survived the trip and were safe!

In the days after we left Pensacola, we got some news, but it was sketchy. The Naval Air Station where Tim worked had been literally destroyed. His office building was hit by a very large wave, and his office, on the first floor, was inundated by eight feet of water.

We received a report from a neighbor that Tim and Shani's house had lost its chimney, and the garage had been damaged—but Fireball, the family fish, came through the storm and its aftermath unscathed!

"...it was a mystery as to who—
or what—this inhabitant was."

Bucky Boomer

Shelley Cabell Moore

There's a creek running through the greenbelt behind our home in the Seattle, Washington, area with large alder, hemlock, and fir trees on the banks. Over the years, my husband, Roy, and I have had visits from opossums, raccoons, and a variety of birds, including hummingbirds, woodpeckers, and stellar blue jays. Once, even a majestic red-tailed hawk landed on our deck rail for a short stopover. But, back in the late 1980s, we had a visit from a creature we'd never seen or heard of before.

On returning from our holiday vacation to see our families in Oregon, Roy surveyed our backyard as he always does after we've been out of town. We've had several very large trees fall down in our yard from the greenbelt during windstorms over the years, and also many a large branch come down, so a check is always in order.

We had bought a living Christmas tree for the first time, and before we left on our trip, Roy planted it in the back yard, just inside the fence on our property line at the edge of the greenbelt. Upon checking on the young, six-foot fir tree, he noticed that all the branches on the bottom foot or so were gone, apparently sawed off, and removed from the yard.

His first thought was that one of the neighborhood kids had gotten a toy saw for Christmas and given it a trial run. After checking with the families on our cul-desac, he found we were the only ones on the street with a tree with "sawed off" lower branches.

About a week later, Roy found all the lower branches had been removed from our ten-foot cedar tree as well, and they were also nowhere to be seen. He then discovered a large hole in the ground just outside the fence in the greenbelt. There was obviously a new neighbor in the area, but it was a mystery as to who—or what—this inhabitant was.

That evening, we were both out in the backyard when we heard a rustling sound in the bushes. I stood still while Roy stealthily worked his way toward the noise.

Standing very quietly, we both watched in amazement as a large, furry, guinea pig-sized critter, with no visible tail, ran over to the fir tree, swiftly climbed it, and began gnawing off a branch. Roy calmly moved to put himself on the path between the fir tree and the hole he'd discovered, placed his hands on his hips, and planted his feet apart, firmly on the ground— thinking he was blocking its escape.

The critter didn't miss a beat. It scurried back down the tree with the branch in its teeth and ran right between Roy's legs, under the fence, and down into its hole. All we could do was laugh at the audacity of the small creature.

Since neither of us had ever seen an animal like it before, we did some research to identify it. It turned out our new resident was a mountain beaver, also known as a sewellel, or boomer. We discovered most people don't even know they exist—which made us feel a whole lot less ignorant.

Mountain beaver are a primitive rodent species, not really beavers, but called so because they also gnaw bark off limbs. They live in the Pacific Northwest from sea level to the tree line. They're about twelve to fourteen inches long, weigh about one to two pounds, are herbivores, are generally slow moving, and have small eyes and ears, long whiskers, a stumpy tail, and sharp teeth. They dig their homes to include six- to eight-inch diameter tunnels with multiple chambers and exits.

Roy and I agreed our little invader was kind of cute, and we named him Bucky Boomer. But, after several more rounds of ornamental plant destruction, he had to go. Not only did Bucky prune the lower branches from two of our young trees, but he also began trimming all of our rhododendrons and azaleas, and our next-door neighbors' shrubs, too.

Roy, the engineer, began to form a plan. He didn't want to hurt Bucky—just catch and release the little critter somewhere safe and away from our backyard and the greenbelt behind us.

Roy's first attempt at capture was simple. He placed a rope with a loop at the end of it around Bucky's large entrance hole, planning to snare the critter as he came out. He held the end of the rope as he sat patiently in a lawn chair in our yard one evening at twilight—since we'd found out during our research that mountain beaver are predominantly nocturnal. After waiting in silence for nearly an hour and a half with no luck, Roy finally gave up.

Next, Roy stuffed black plastic, dirt, and rocks in the hole he'd found, hoping to force Bucky to move on to greener pastures, unaware at the time of the numerous entrances and exits mountain beaver build in their territory. This too failed.

Upon discovering another hole Bucky had dug, Roy became even more determined in his efforts to capture him. It was time to build a full-fledged trap. A trip to the library aided Roy in finding a diagram and instructions for building a large box trap with a drop down door to seal Bucky inside.

He spent his first free weekend constructing it with one-inch plywood. He marked, sawed, nailed, and completed his sturdy wooden trap. The door was lifted and secured, and a ripe, juicy apple was skewered inside as bait. The trap was set and strategically placed, and each morning, Roy faithfully checked it.

For several weeks, Roy watched and waited, changing out the apple for a fresh one several times. Then, early one morning, he found the trap sprung. Peeking carefully inside, he saw the apple was gone, the stick it was impaled on was chewed up, and Bucky was cowering in a corner in the back of the box.

Roy was ecstatic! He called our neighbor, Jeff, and the two of them carried the trap out to the car and loaded it into the trunk. Roy and Jeff drove out to a forested area with no houses, took the trap from the trunk, carried it into the woods, and set it down. Bucky began hissing and running around inside the trap, so the two men very carefully lifted the door, standing aside to avoid a confrontation.

As soon as Bucky realized he had a way out of his predicament, he ran out of the trap and off into the brush, without hesitation. Roy and Jeff carried the empty trap back to the car and headed home feeling relieved and satisfied.

The mystery of the missing tree branches had been solved, and the perpetrator had been caught unharmed and relocated to a larger territory where he could live in comfort for the remainder of his days. Our furry menace was now gone and our trees and shrubs no longer in jeopardy.

There was no chance Bucky could ever find his way back to our yard. Only one question remained. Might Bucky Boomer still have relatives living in our greenbelt?

Shelley Cabell Moore was born in Oregon City, Oregon. She is an Oregon State University graduate and a former elementary school teacher. Shelley married her high school sweetheart, LeRoy, a test engineer for Boeing, and they raised their daughter in the same Seattle, Washington area home where they encountered Bucky Boomer. Shelley enjoys spending time with her family, reading, writing, and traveling to experience different countries and cultures.

"...I ran 365 days with zero days missed."

Quest for 3,000

Dan Heiner

About seven and a half years ago, I got a call from my high school cross-country track coach. He wanted me to come and race the high school cross-country team in the Astoria Annual Alumni Meet.

I thought, *What the heck—I've got two weeks to prepare.*

Of course, I'd graduated twenty-seven years before and not done any running at all since—too busy working. My first day of training was to be four miles. Two out. Two back.

About a half hour after daylight, I started up the logging road behind my house. About one and a half miles out, my legs said, "You go ahead. We're not going with you!"

After two weeks, I could do four miles without stopping. A few days before the alumni race, I got muscle cramps in my calves. On race day, I ran with my calves still locked tight and finished next to last—about twenty minutes for two and a half miles. That was September 1997.

In December '97, I decided to shoot for April 1998 and the Trail's End Marathon. My younger brother, Don, had run the race in 1974 and finished in three hours, eleven minutes. Being forty-three years old, I decided that was the time to beat. With four months of running training, I completed my first marathon in three hours and fifty-five minutes.

I continued to run. I finished the Portland Marathon

in October '98 in three hours and twenty-one minutes. The hunt was on! I finished 1998 with two marathons and one 10k—1,338 miles overall.

I started 1999 with the goal of 2,000 miles and running both marathons. I made it three marathons and three 10ks. My best marathon time was three hours and sixteen minutes—still my best time. By the end of '99, I finished with 2,200 miles—forty-two miles a week on average.

In 2000, I ran two marathons, three 10ks, and the Hood to Coast Relay—2,111 miles, forty miles a week on average.

The year 2001 included a 20k, three 10ks, and one marathon—with 2,042 miles, or thirty-nine miles a week on average.

My goal for 2002 was fifty miles average a week and 2,600 miles total. I finished the year with 2,530 miles and a forty-eight miles a week average—three 10k races, two marathons, and one half-marathon.

Missing my goal of an average of fifty miles a week upset me. I'd missed sixty-two days for the year. If I'd have just run only two miles a day more, I would have beat my goal, and then some.

For 2003, the goal? No mercy—fifty miles average per week, for 2,600 miles. I found out the first week that by running seven days a week, I could do sixty miles pretty easily. Wanting to stay ahead of my goal, that's what I did. Sixty miles in seven days.

Hammering away all year, it came to me that with a sixty-mile average, 3,000 miles was in range. I finished the year with two marathons, one 20k, four 10ks, the Hood to Coast Relay, and a total for the year of 3,148 miles. Plus, I ran 365 days with zero days missed.

I moved on in 2004, shooting for seven days a week and a fifty-mile average. On December 11, I turned fifty years old. Forty-nine was just fine, but fifty was nifty. Run on! I finished the year with four 10ks, one 15k, one marathon, a fifty-mile average, and a total of 2,602 miles.

On January 1, 2005, I looked up my totals from the

past seven years. Adding up all my miles, I found I had run 15,971 miles!

1998 - 1,338 miles
1999 - 2,200 miles
2000 - 2,111 miles
2001 - 2,042 miles
2002 - 2,530 miles
2003 - 3,148 miles
2004 - 2,602 miles

So, off I went again.

On January 4, 2005, I reached 16,000 miles! My new goal was fifty miles a week, including trying to take a few days off.

Barring injuries—which I've been lucky with so far—I hope to make 20,000 miles by the end of 2006.

On December 31, 2006, Dan Heiner logged in a total of 20,718 miles, surpassing his goal—just in time!

"...there was so much pain, I was on the brink of passing out."

Emily's September Fall

Emily Rummel

As you come into Oxbow, Oregon, Copperfield Park is just below Oxbow Dam. It's warm and quiet, the water runs green, and the air is crisp and fresh smelling.

There were just the four of us—two friends, John and Sheryl, and my husband, Bruce, and me. No children. The men liked to fish for catfish, small mouth bass, blue gill, and crappie. Sheryl and I planned to mostly sit in a little camp spot and read.

Eastern Oregon and Idaho had just finished summer break, so no teenagers were around, which meant everyone in the RV park was probably at least fifty. It was early September, a really quiet time of year, and we didn't think we'd need a reservation, but when we got there, the grounds were full. We had to park up above at Oxbow Dam on a wide spot at the side of the hill.

The next morning, we got up early and sat around drinking coffee until I decided the day was too beautiful to waste. I walked over to the top of the bank where I could see fish in the river, about fifty feet below. I wanted to get a closer look at those fish.

Actually, I was looking forward to fishing once or twice with Bruce. I hadn't fished since I was a kid. I really knew little about nature, as I was into horses— riding trails mostly.

Down over the bank, I saw a nice little trail. It looked firm, so I took a couple steps. The ground gave way like loose sand. I quickly reached down to grab a bush, not realizing I was basically suspended over nothing. It was like standing on a diving board. Nothing was beneath my feet.

I leaned forward and reached for anything solid. I grabbed for a branch but missed it as my body hurtled past. I flipped three times in the air and landed face down in a huge bush thirty feet below.

As I flew through the air, I somehow missed an enormous boulder, only clipping my ankle. But I did hit my head on something, because I had a big red mark on my forehead, and perhaps, as I was flying, I hit my wrist and forearm. The wrist was all popped weird and was very painful. I'm a nurse's assistant, so I was pretty sure it wasn't broken—probably just dislocated.

I rolled over on the bush. If it hadn't been there, I would have been dead. I quietly tried to collect my wits.

I was so embarrassed by my fall. My husband had just told me to be careful, and I didn't want anyone to see me looking like a fool. Besides, there was so much pain, I was on the brink of passing out. I sat up, then remained there, motionless.

Fortunately, Bruce, Sheryl, and John had heard my thunk—probably as I ricocheted past the boulder. Later, they described it as sounding like a ripe watermelon smashing to bits on something solid.

They came rapidly down a stable trail to rescue me. They were glad I was still alive, but there was no way they could carry me back up. They decided there were two choices: call a helicopter, or Bruce and John could shove me up the trail.

Who knows how long a helicopter would take after it was called. Besides, the bush wasn't really a safe place to stay. So, Sheryl scurried on ahead. With the two fellows pushing from behind, we slowly made it back up.

The pain in my wrist and arm was excruciating! My body wanted to pass out, but I wouldn't allow it. I remained conscious and on my feet clear to the top.

Thankfully, Sheryl had a big bucket of ice and water waiting for me. Gratefully, I stuck my arm in clear up to the elbow and kept it there while everyone else gathered up the coffee things.

We took both vehicles. Ours was a Ford pickup 4x4 with a fifth-wheel trailer, and John and Sheryl's was a Dodge with a travel trailer. We quickly drove down to the camp and got our rigs situated next to each other.

While they were unhooking the fifth-wheel from our truck, I decided to crawl in and gather enough clothing so I could change from my torn and dirty outfit to look decent for the hospital trip. When I took my hand out of the ice, the feeling and all the pain came back. It was intolerable!

I grabbed my right hand with my left, pulled and twisted, and heard and felt a loud POP! The extreme pain was gone. I only ached all over fairly equally then.

Except for being slightly red from contact with the bush, my face had been spared, though there was a small scratch on the bridge of my nose. I struggled into something clean.

My husband drove as fast as the conditions of the winding, narrow road would allow. It was about an hour's ride through the beautiful, scenic mountains. I wish I could have enjoyed the trip.

Bruce knew I was hurting, though I'm the type that doesn't complain much. He was especially worried about my ankle and wrist. Both of them were swollen to at least twice their normal size.

Bruce knew where to find the closest hospital—Baker City—because he hunted and fished in that area all the time. It was open, and the staff was very friendly.

After an exam and an X-ray, the doctor announced, "Nothing broken!"

We could hardly believe it.

The four of us drove back to our campsite, and I sat around for a full week being waited on hand and foot—and reading. What did I read? Oh, I'd brought a combination of things: inspirational, mystery, Harlequin romance, and plenty of Muriel Jensen's books.

I took that time just to refocus on life. By the time we

left, I had gotten my fill of reading.

But I did enjoy the weather. It was beautiful. Hot, no wind, the trees were still green, and the sun shone every day, with only an occasional cloud. And, no, I wasn't tempted even once to check out the fish.

Emily Rummel was born and raised in the Lewis and Clark area next to Astoria, Oregon. Her husband, Bruce, worked for the Oregon Department of Transportation on Highway Maintenance. When their children were grown and the house became somewhat empty, Emily went back to work as a Certified Nursing Assistant in the Lower Columbia Clinic. She is now retired.

"...one can't help but become intimately in touch with the river's pulse..."

Little Romance in Dispatching Routines

Dan Butler

The rowdy, colorful days of dispatching river pilots from a smoke-filled room on Portland, Oregon's, boisterous waterfront are long gone. Whatever romance is left on the river now flows unseen and unnoticed past the Columbia River Pilots' land-locked office in the midst of a totally unromantic industrial park. At least that's the opinion of this rather contemporary pilot dispatcher, who can't even see the river from his desk, let alone the mast of a ship.

Nestled in the sterile landscape of busy warehouses on North Portland's Lombard Street, our tidy and professional little building looks more like a mosque or a 7-Eleven store than the nerve center for all ship movements on the Columbia.

Yet, from this utilitarian setting, the wanderings of every vessel requiring a pilot is monitored as it arrives, departs, or shifts around the river. Our office is the hub of all vessel traffic information, and most orders for pilots originate on my desk.

The place has served as my daytime residence ten hours a day, two weeks each month, throughout the past eighteen years. Even with this tenure, I'm still the "junior" man and work the second half of every month, while senior dispatcher, Al Onkka, works the first half.

Together, with our counterparts—Larry Allen and Ed Steve at the Columbia River Bar Pilots station in Astoria, Oregon—we coordinate the piloting needs of the river's shipping industry 365 days a year.

The job of dispatching pilots is a very simple concept: provide a rested, state-licensed pilot for all foreign-flagged vessels transiting the river. In practice, it's a little more complex and involves numerous other functions as well. And, like many jobs in the transportation business, the routine can vary from sheer boredom to intense concentration, depending on the volume of traffic and the frequency of unexpected crises.

My day at the Portland office begins shortly before 0700 when I update all the activity that occurred during the previous evening, as reported by the Merchant's Exchange. Although this information is tracked in our computer, we manually note ship movements and pilot locations on a large display board with hooks and tags.

As it looks like something from a World War II plotting room, I like to refer to it as 100 years of tradition unmarred by progress. Vintage qualities aside, the board is a most effective way of showing the status of every ship, dock, anchorage, and pilot at a glance.

After setting the board and updating the computer, I begin making calls to the various berths where ships are being worked to determine their schedule for the next twenty-four hours. This gives me an early indication of the day's tentative sailing or shifting activity. Armed with my rough estimates, best guesses, hunches, and gut feelings, I make my first call to the Astoria office at 0815.

Larry, my counterpart in Astoria, sits in the catbird seat. His office faces the Columbia Bay where he can look out through windows, desk-to-ceiling on the riverside, with water sloshing the pilings below. Something is always passing by—huge container ships, cruise ships, tour boats, pleasure yachts, sternwheelers, skiffs, scows, sailboats, speedboats, sailboards, kayaks, tugs, barges, sea lions, a very occasional killer whale, and the pilot launches. Along with helicopters, herons, or cormorants swooping low over the river, Larry's view is never dull.

My 0815 call is the first of three planning calls that Larry and I have each day to go over ship movements. Typically, I'll provide the Columbia River Bar with all initial orders for ships arriving and sailing, while Larry updates me with new ETAs (military for "expected time of arrival") that he has received directly from inbound ships approaching the Bar to travel into the river.

Traditionally, ships contacted the bar pilot office with arrival times via the ship's wireless, hence the term "ships' wire." Today, with e-mail, cell phones, and satellite communication, wires have become all but obsolete.

We also discuss arrival, or sailing windows, for those ships with deep drafts of over thirty-six feet. If there are more inbounds than there are rested pilots, I let Larry know when I'll be sending more down. Likewise, if there are more pilots in Astoria than arrivals, I'll "pull" the pilots by car and return them to the bottom of the Portland board. We have to give the pilots two hours' notice, three if they're coming from Longview, Washington.

The Longview dispatcher has control of the company's cars and will send cars downriver with needed pilots or will send empty cars down to pull back pilots needed upriver. Bar pilots used to have to catch public buses to make their schedules—so the company cars are one improvement over the past.

After our morning call, both the bar and river pilots will have a rough idea of the next twenty-four hours' activity. While it's not the most accurate information at that early hour, it is the best info available. We now have a place to start planning the rest of the day.

At 0830, I record the first of four pilot tapes, which I make throughout the day to provide callers with a schedule of vessel movements. It also lists every pilot's assignment and board position. Prior to the advent of the Internet, this tape was the primary means for pilots to determine when they could expect their next assignment. Tug companies, the Lines Bureau, stevedores—the dock workers that load and unload cargo—and steamship agents continue to use this recording method to aid in planning their activities.

After the hectic crunch of trying to complete the morning plan for the 0830 tape, it's time to begin calling the steamship agents when they arrive at their offices. By mid-morning, they'll have a fair idea of how their ships will be worked in terms of hiring longshore labor, loading issues, and the arrival of cargo by train. They will also update us with ETAs of the arriving ships that we began tracking about four days out.

By 1030, it's time for our second Astoria call, where Larry and I can further refine the day's activities. At 1100, I put out the second tape.

While dispatching pilots throughout the day, I continue to put more shine on an increasingly polished plan for the coming night's activity. I call the Bar with form or "set" sailing times, notice of new arrivals, and ETA changes, and I check on whether or not we need to send or pull pilots.

The day progresses with faxes, e-mails, and constant phone or Nextel radio calls. In resolving the myriad of minor and major details involved in keeping ships moving, one can't help but become intimately in touch with the river's pulse on any given day.

Although dispatchers don't actually control the ships—that's the pilot's job—no transit occurs without our guidance and scheduling. We also manage the designated anchorages in Astoria, Longview, and Vancouver, Washington, allocating them according to vessel size, draft, and projected availability.

Since the office is not manned after 1700, all orders for after-hour ship movements are determined by 1600 each day. The day's second crunch then begins as I make the last Astoria call to advise Larry of which ships are sailing when and with whom.

After our call is fully completed, it's time to spring into action and dispatch pilots for the evening's sailings and harbor jobs. I prepare a final fax for the Exchange and record the last tape of the day at 1630. By 1700, it's game over and time to forward the phones to home, where I'll be on call until morning when I return and start it all over again.

Obviously, ship scheduling isn't a very romantic operation these days. Maybe it never was. I tend to see it more like a timed puzzle that starts every day at 0700 and must be successfully completed by 1700. It isn't a question of if or when you'll solve the dispatch puzzle. It's simply how good you are at finding a solution—and there's *always* a solution. It's just that some are much better than others. The irony of my career didn't really strike me until after I'd been here for some time.

When I was a youngster growing up in Corvallis, Oregon, my folks took us kids on the occasional trek to Portland. On some of those trips, we'd visit the docks and look at the merchant ships. Absolutely fascinated by them, I took note of their often strange and whimsical names, pondering their exotic cargos and wondering the distant ports they'd been to.

Once home, I'd always scan the Sunday paper's port calendar, checking out the posted sailings and arrivals to see if any of those ships had returned to Portland. Little did I know, decades later, I'd become the very person responsible for collecting and distributing the same information.

While dispatchers may not have the high profile or esteemed standing of river pilots, it's interesting and enjoyable work. We are, after all, at the very heart of the action. Put in proper perspective, I look at dispatching like this—the pilots may pilot the ships—but I pilot the pilots.

"It was obviously a toy
that had seen lots of action."

The Magic Marble

Stan Brown

It was late in the fall, and the grounds around our marble factory needed a last mowing before the rain fell and ice formed, or the dormant plants began to come to life. Of course, gophers, moles, and other rodents know not of seasons and continue to aerate, excavate, and pursue the art of mound building while cleaning out tunnels and storerooms for their extensive new explorations and underground works.

My task was to go about leveling and tamping down these soil eruptions to give the mower even terrain for a better-finished look. One mound was exceptionally large, and as it was under the apple tree—a favorite place for lunching and sunset contemplations—got my special attention. After leveling and tamping, I retired for the day with the expectation of mowing after the dew had evaporated the next morning.

Around 10:00 a.m., a brief burst of sun dried the grass enough to mow. The smell of fresh-cut grass, and the smooth operation of the electric mower, lulled me into a comfortable walking pace. Birds singing and distant freeway sounds confirmed all was well with the world—until I arrived at the area under the apple tree.

There, I found a mound, bigger than the day before, in the same spot I had previously cleared. Mumbling to myself about the moles and gophers and their ilk, I released the mower's automatic shut off and stepped forward to clean the fresh disruption—but I was stopped in my tracks.

Atop the unusually large twelve-inch-high, eighteen-inch-diameter mound, rested a vintage five-eighths-inch, reddish-orange puree marble moon—nicks and all. It was obviously a toy that had seen lots of action.

Our marble shop was in a rezoned residential area, and many children could have played with it. My elation at finding the prize prompted me to pick up the wine-colored orb and declare the mound a historical site to be forever undisturbed by boot or mower.

I gave thanks for the truly lucky found marble, a treasure from the distant past.

Stan Brown, known locally as the Marble Guy, owned and operated a marble store in Astoria, Oregon. He relished in giving out "lucky marbles" to people who came into his shop, at local weekend craft markets, and to people he passed on the street. His pockets were always filled with the small glass spheres, and he had a miniature marble museum in his shop. He also enjoyed teaching people how to play marbles.

"I was still conscious,
which meant I was still alive."

My Last Ride
at Speed—Probably

Walt Garnett

Bump? There shouldn't be a bump here.

Thump! Tire squall! Scrape! Fiberglass on pavement!

What fiberglass? My helmet? It's my helmet. On the pavement? I'm on the ground.

Flat out in sixth gear, doing 140-150 miles per hour, and I'm on the ground? I can't be on the ground. I'm too old to be on the ground at this speed. Oh, ##@#, this is going to hurt!

****

I discovered motor racing at the fairly normal age of twelve. Somewhat less normal was that I started driving racing sports and formula cars at age fifteen, which was over forty-five years ago.

The rules of engagement were somewhat different then than now. It was quite common in the 1950s and early '60s for a racer to be the minimum age of twenty-one for three to six years while his true age caught up with the paperwork.

In 1968, I fell passionately in love with road-racing sidecars. A sidecar is a three-wheeled motorcycle, with two wheels in line and the third off to the left side.

The driver controls the throttle, brakes, and steering, and the passenger provides mobile ballast to help the bike turn. The rules do not allow seat belts or other restraints for safety reasons.

I raced as a passenger and as a driver for sixteen years. A crash that tore up too many muscles in my right arm put an end to my sidecar racing just as my son was coming of age, so we went go-kart racing instead.

In 2002, my racing had been on hold for a couple of years for financial reasons, but the passion still burned. Circumstances put me in contact with an old, but still active, sidecar-racing buddy.

One thing led to another, and I borrowed some old leathers from him and started passengering again. Mutual recommendations teamed me with a very good driver, and I began having way too much fun—*again*.

Pacific Raceway, near Aurora, Washington, is a wonderful facility. Its two miles of twisting asphalt go up hill, down dale, and through a glen, much like a fairy tale. It's almost more fun than a passenger can stand. It even has a slight bend to the right, near the end of the long front straight, which isn't actually very straight at all. They call this bend the dogleg, or turn one.

In June of 2003, my regular driver was absent, so I talked my way into riding with another outfit—one whose driver was not so highly recommended. But, I wanted to race, and I figured I could handle it. I always could before.

About halfway through the race, we were rocketing through the dogleg when I felt a bump that shouldn't have been there. I found out later that my driver had cut off another sidecar, and we'd hit them. They, in turn, bounced off the nearby retaining wall and slammed back into us—with a loud thump.

The thump tossed me off the platform, and I somehow wound up in front of our bike. We'd been speeding along at about 145 miles per hour, and my driver tried frantically to stop, causing the tires to squall—which occurs when they're abused, such as during heavy braking or getting too far sideways.

The bike kept nudging me into sideways rolls on the

pavement, as we had a lot of momentum to slow from before we stopped. I was sliding along on my left side, still tucked into the fetal position I used to stay out of the wind, when my worldview darkened as I rolled over onto my face.

The pavement was flying by almost too fast to recognize. Then, my view lightened again briefly as I completed the roll. Sadly, I rolled again, faster, and again, and again. Light, dark, light, dark.

Darn!

When you hit the ground at high speed, sliding is better than tumbling. The leather suits we wear are designed to guard against abrasions, but they don't work that well against impacts.

Yes, you can get severe burns and scrapes from sliding along on the pavement, but you don't generally break things. Tumbling is another matter. At such a high speed, your muscles can't hold a tuck, and you flail. And when an outstretched arm or leg comes back around to pound the pavement, it often breaks.

My tumbling abruptly stopped for some reason, which left me flat on my back and sliding. This was much better. I got into the gravel and dust at the edge of the pavement just before I finally stopped.

I was still conscious, which meant I was still alive. I thought these were two very good signs!

I lay there for a few seconds, amazed that nothing seemed to hurt. Of course, I had to be in shock, and adrenaline is a wonderful painkiller, so what did I know?

I did know better than to try to get up. I at least knew that much. So, I started to count and wiggle things instead: neck, knees, elbows, shoulders, hips, hands, feet.

As I moved each body part in turn, I was looking for a response and for sharp, stabbing pain. The pain indicates something is seriously bent. No response is worse.

The only casualty seemed to be that my left index finger and its mate wouldn't move. *Not bad.*

Not bad? Absolutely amazing!

A shadow moved between my face and the sun, shading my head. It was someone standing over me. I couldn't see who it was, but someone was there. Another good sign.

Then, I heard voices telling me not to move.

I quipped, "I know about that, I've done this before."

Then, I realized the reason I couldn't see anything clearly was that I didn't have my glasses on.

I asked, "Has anyone seen my glasses?" and someone said they'd look.

About the time my glasses were found and placed on my face, the EMTs arrived. I'd been talking with the corner workers and the other sidecar crew—the one we'd hit.

Corner workers are a wonderful cadre of volunteers who work at safety stations set up at each corner and use a system of colored flags to warn the racers of hazardous situations on the racetrack. They also assist the emergency crews in the case of an accident.

I thought I recognized the other passenger's voice, but I wasn't sure. I asked someone to unfasten my helmet strap, and that made it a lot easier to breathe.

Then I asked, "Is everyone else okay?" and was assured, "They're all just fine."

The EMTs asked me about my neck, and, "Does anything hurt?" Their chief concerns are always neck and back injuries.

I was euphoric that I hadn't broken anything major. At least nothing I knew about.

They wanted to start taking off my protective gear, but their version of the right way was with scissors. I was wearing about $1,500 worth of someone else's leather suit, and scissors were not on my list.

My left hand was a bit messy, and the two fingers still wouldn't move—I thought they were broken for sure. Everything else seemed fine. So, I talked them into just helping me remove things. I helped them put me onto a gurney, and they loaded me up for the ride to Aurora Hospital and a forced overnight stay.

Would I go back to racing again? I doubted it. Just ten days before the trip, I'd celebrated my sixtieth birthday.

Maybe it was finally time to stop racing. *Maybe.* But, then again, I didn't break anything. All I had were sprains, scrapes, and bruises. Lots of bruises.

One hundred forty-five miles per hour, and nothing broken! Whoever was up there watching over me, thank you. Thank you very much!

Walt Garnett was the author of the computer how-to book, Garbage In, Gorgeous Out, *and nine works written and published for non-profit organizations. He and his wife lived in Astoria, Oregon, and occasionally worked in Portland and Seattle. Walt kept numerous pets, none of which ate very much, because they were all confirmed artificials and quite stuffed. Walt left this world in June 2017.*

"Fishermen are always ready.
It's in their blood."

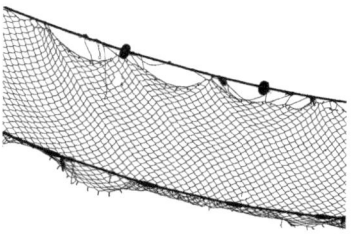

The Day Flood

Alfred H. Olson

Columbia River gillnetting was a culture all to itself. Unfortunately, memories are about all that's left of this occupation. In the late 1950s, when I wasn't yet twenty, I spent a day gillnetting on the lower Columbia River.

As the sun began to settle in the western sky at the end of a warm August day, my skipper, Don Riswick, and I left the mooring and began our journey down to the middle of Sand Island. The ebb tide made a dark low-water possible, and we were—like many others—ready.

The plan was to make a drift or two—and possibly a third—that would see us drift around Point Ellis, there being no bridge at the time, and pick up in a part of the river known as the Blind Channel. During the first drift, we got twelve fish. The second, we got twenty.

"There must be a few around," we agreed.

Our third drift saw ten more twenty-pound Chinook salmon come over the side.

As the last end of the net came into the boat, we began to think of where we would anchor up to prepare for the always imposing and sleep-robbing day flood. Nobody much liked them, but few chose to miss them. The season was short, and we would be out there if there were fish around.

After a brief discussion, Don and I decided to tie up at the floating dock at the Megler Ferry Landing. This would give us time to get breakfast before the day flood,

186

the first of two floods each day, corresponding to the tides. But first, we needed some sleep. Even a few hours are better than none.

The bunks in our little twenty-six-foot double-ender were marginal—at best—but when you're tired, most anything will do. Comfort was aided by the heat generated by the dependable, fifty-horsepower Gray engine that had gotten us so many places for so many years.

There was something about the sights and smells of that little twenty-six-footer that are still vivid today. I liked fishing. I liked being on the boat, and those memories linger.

As I was dozing off, I heard the sound of the exhaust from my dad's twenty-eight-footer, *SANDY-CEE*, coming in to tie up on the outside of ours. His exhaust really made lots of noise when the square-stern boat was at high speed, but now it was comparatively quiet.

Dad had my cousin, Eldred Olson, with him, and they were going day flooding too. Cousin Eldred was a grown man. Not only could he do his share of the work on the much larger boat, but he also got half the earnings. I was learning the ropes on the much smaller boat and got a much smaller percentage.

Too soon, the alarm rang. Our four-hour nap was over. It was time for breakfast. Don and I walked up to the Megler Ferry Landing restaurant for a bite to eat.

Guess who was there? My dad and my cousin. How they got from their boat across our boat so quietly, and to the dock, I'll never know.

Conversation over breakfast included a few pull-tabs. I was too young to do that, but no one seemed to care. After our meal, we headed back to the boat.

Dad pulled out first, then we fired up and let our dependable little four-banger—its four-cylinder engine—get us to the middle of Sand Island for our first drift. Don's boat didn't have a name, only numbers, and now, over fifty years later, I don't recall what they were.

By the time we laid out the net, I was wide awake

and ready. Fishermen are always ready. It's in their blood.

This drift netted ten fish. The second drift, fifteen. After picking up for the fifth time in twenty-four hours, we trusted our little four-banger to get us over Taylor Sands and into port. She always came through.

After delivering our fish and getting fuel, we once again headed for home. We talked over arrangements for the next evening's fishing, and Don dropped me off at my house.

"See you at nine o'clock. Get some good sleep," he said.

A real bed was going to feel great after a hard day's work.

Alfred H. Olson was born in Astoria, Oregon in 1938. He attended Oregon College of Education, graduating in 1961. After college, Al served in the U.S. Army before he started teaching and coaching at Warrenton High School. In 1969, he began teaching and coaching at Astoria High School until his retirement in 1999. Al is a weekly volunteer at the Columbia River Maritime Museum. When he isn't busy volunteering, he enjoys sport fishing and golf. He and his wife have traveled extensively in the U.S., in Canada, and abroad.

"Chai's attitude was always quite unrepentant."

Chai and the Critters

Pat Williams

Anyone who's lived with outdoor avid hunter cats knows well the unexpected surprises these cats will bring their people. Whether it's a, "See what a great hunter I am?" or "Here! This is in payment for the warm lap you let me sit on," or "Hee, hee, here's another surprise!" these cats never allow your life to get dull.

If there were a competition for Best Hunter, Chai, our resident great hunter cat, would definitely have been in the running. Chai opted to come live with us due to unresolved conflicts with the family who thought they owned her.

When she moved in, she immediately established her dominance over our other two cats, Mr. Kitty and Miss Kitty. These two more easy-going cats were perfectly content to sit in some high places, watching Chai's antics.

A short time after moving in, Chai returned to her old home and stole a plump little hen to the chagrin of her somewhat miffed owner. Chai's attitude was always quite unrepentant.

I'm sure given another opportunity, she'd surely have repeated the offense. Fortunately, her former owners moved out of the area, and although there were no more bantam hens to steal, Chai continued bringing us both living and dead offerings, be it snakes, squirrels, shrews, voles, moles, young wharf rats, or mice.

Since she beat us down with piercing yowls and

shredded screens, a cat door was usually left open for her to come and go at will. So, there was no warning about what would appear in front of her favorite offering spot, the rug in the bathroom. Consequently, before using the facilities, it wasn't unusual to have to first remove the spoils—alive or in pieces.

Usually, there was some time between offerings, but the last week of September 2011, Chai went all out and started the week with a live mouse. The next day, it was a snake, and then the remains of a rat. By Thursday, we were getting a little leery of going into the bathroom without cautiously checking the rug first.

Friday morning, I was working at the computer when I heard furious squeaking and scuffling sounds from the bathroom. When I apprehensively went to check, there was Chai, standing at full alert on the edge of the small rug, watching a rather significant unmoving lump underneath it.

Not knowing what it was but thinking it was still alive—because of the noises it had been making just moments before—I cautiously stepped closer and grabbed Chai, took her out, and closed the bathroom door. I then put her outside and secured the house.

I thought the critter, whatever it was, would eventually come out from under the rug, and I went back to what I'd been doing before the interruption. Actually, in the back of my mind, I was trying to figure out how I was going to find out what it was without having to lift up the rug to see.

An hour or so later, I needed to get ready to leave for an appointment, when suddenly, I remembered I'd not yet dealt with the lump. I cautiously opened the bathroom door, and, yep, there was the lump—still under the rug but in a different spot.

Now what am I going to do?

I found a small cardboard box and put it over the lump and weighted it down with the closest thing at hand, a fully-loaded school backpack. I brushed my teeth and washed up, opting to take a shower later.

The entire time, it was like an elephant was in the room. I couldn't just ignore the stack of stuff on the rug and not find out what was underneath it.

So, deciding I needed something thin to slide under everything so the box could be flipped over to carry outside, I managed to find an old piece of siding and carefully worked it under the rug and the box.

When I thought I'd gotten it under whatever critter was there, I carefully lifted up the box and looked.

Nope. Just a little more.

I flipped the box, agitating whatever the lump was, causing more angry squeaking. I cautiously carried the box, board, rug, and critter out the door and across the yard to some low ground cover.

Setting the box down, I lifted the board off. There it was. The "really scary creature" was a very large, and very angry, mole. I laughed and carefully turned the box on its side so the highly indignant and very vocal critter could beat a hasty retreat.

Our family decided that from then on, limited access to the house was best for Chai. When she indicated she wanted in, we checked her out thoroughly before allowing entrance.

She didn't particularly like it, and we were at her beck and call, but it worked better for us. At least our nerves appreciated it.

"...I couldn't understand how people dared to venture out on foot.."

Where My Adventure Shoes Took Me

Wynne Preston

While shopping for cross-trainers for my trip to Ireland, the clerk informed me I was actually looking for an adventure shoe. That was food for thought.

It was the summer of 1990, and I was almost twenty-six years old. I was leaving my fiancé in California and heading off to do a summer internship for part of my social work program. I was going for a Master's degree and feeling as though I was a master of nothing. I was scared to death.

Considering that one of my classmates was going to India and did not even speak the language, Ireland should have felt like a piece of cake. But thinking that way can get you into trouble.

On the surface, visiting a country where English is spoken can appear to be no challenge. Things, people, and situations seem familiar to you, similar to what you might be used to as an American. But, there's a lot more than what meets the eye.

One example of this is the language. I watched the movie *My Left Foot* beforehand, for a crash course on the Irish accent. I left the theater feeling overwhelmed and wondering what I had gotten myself into.

I discovered that regional Irish dialects could range from a slight accent to completely incomprehensible. Add to that the fact that some of my clients-to-be had mental health problems and were not the most articulate people in the world—eeek!

Another point of confusion was the slang expressions. One day after my arrival early in the summer, I was to meet my supervisor at a client's house—a typical row house lining a narrow street.

The client offered tea several times, but when I continued to demur, she gave me a scrutinizing look and said to my supervisor, "Frankly, she looks pissed!"

Lest you think she meant "upset" or "angry," I found out, to my chagrin, that she meant "drunk" instead.

Another time, a friend mentioned going to the hole in the wall.

"Oh, I've been to that restaurant," I said, thinking she was talking about The Hole In the Wall, a restaurant in Dublin I had enjoyed.

She laughed and said, "I mean the place where you get money."

When she asked for the American term, I provided, "ATM." In response to her blank look, I filled in, "Automated Teller Machine."

She laughed again and commented, "Yes, Americans would call them that."

There were a lot of preconceived notions about Americans, too.

For instance, one day when I showed up early, having given myself extra time because I was going someplace new and was not familiar with the bus route, someone said to me, "Oh, yeah, I forgot you Americans have a problem with time."

Riding the bus was an adventure all in itself. The streets were often very narrow, and all drivers, without exception, seemed to drive them like the high scorer on a kid's video game. While I don't know Irish driving laws, the concept of the pedestrian having the right of way seemed completely lost on them.

Watching the near mayhem through the window increased my stress level but certainly distracted me from motion sickness. I was sure I was going to witness a death, and I couldn't understand how people dared to venture out on foot. After crossing the street one time, I actually had a black mark on my leg from the front bumper of an impatient car.

Another driving adventure involved a visit to the Cliffs of Moher, one of the most stunning vistas I have ever seen. The cliffs, located on the west coast of Ireland, make a staggering vertical drop to the sea, and the sheer scale of them dwarfs the solitary traveler.

Our schedule was tight. Consequently, our Irish driver was anxious to get there quickly, insisting we had just enough time if we hurried. He drove with the zeal and disregard for our mortality that seemed universal in Ireland. The two-lane roads were all very narrow, both lanes together barely wider than the car we were in. Many of the roads were closed, so we often had to turn around and forge another route.

Also, since the Cliffs of Moher are a popular tourist attraction, we frequently happened upon large tour buses. When we came upon one of these monstrosities, our driver slammed on his brakes and drove up into the fields in order to let the bus pass. It loomed over us as it drove by, sometimes only inches from our wide eyes. I was not surprised when my travel companion asked if I would trade and ride in the front seat on the way home.

The biggest adventure of the whole trip was my bicycle tour to a remote area at the end of the summer. I prepared for the strenuous route by exercising every night after work. My favorite effort was walking on the beach. Whenever it was low tide, I could walk far out onto the bare shore. I played my Walkman, sang as loud as I wanted, and looked out at the sea.

As much as I tried to be ready for the tour, my efforts were not enough to fully prepare me for the twenty-five- to forty-two-mile daily legs over rolling hills and bumpy roads. We cyclists quickly divided ourselves into two groups.

An eleven-year-old girl, her mother, and I made up the slow group. There was also a nice middle-aged gentleman who often hung out with us. We saw him pass everyone else one time on a sizable hill, so he must have just preferred our company.

One time, when the four of us were crashing—I mean taking a break—along a roadside next to a field with both cows and castle ruins (not an uncommon sight on this trip) I got the most wonderful feeling. We were totally isolated, unreachable. Just us and the land—and what a beautiful land.

Throughout that summer, I met wonderful people who had a genuineness and simplicity uncommon at home. Even though I had always thought of the American West Coast as relaxed, I learned ways to slow down even more. I now realize that a good adventure doesn't necessarily need an exotic locale, just an open mind—and perhaps a good pair of adventure shoes.

Wynne Preston is a child and family therapist, and she has enjoyed writing since she was young. She was born in Nuremberg, Germany, of American parents. Aside from Europe and her current home in Astoria, Oregon, she has lived on the East Coast, in the Midwest and on the West Coast, which is the area she resonates with most. Wynne's current adventures include being married, raising two adventurous daughters, giving talks at her church, training for a one-mile swim across the Columbia River, and starting her first private practice. Although her work is important, her true career is life!

"The kid didn't want to tell
his parents the whole story."

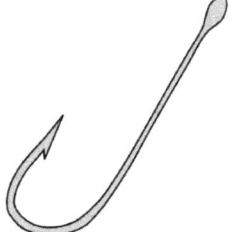

Kid Overboard

Walt Receconi

My dad and I used to commercial fish in Alaska, and
we were up at Turnagain Arm in Prince William Sound
in 1981. Dad and I were gillnetting in our stem picker we
called the *Gracie R.* We had our net out and were sitting
in the pilothouse just killing time, reading magazines.

Suddenly, my dad asked, "Did you hear something?"

I answered, "No," and we went back to reading.

After a couple minutes, Dad asked again, and I said
no, again. When it happened a third time, we got up and
started looking around. The closest boat to us was
around 300 yards away. It was another gillnetter, a bow
reeler—the kind we referred to as floating coffins—and
it sat to our stern. They're really small, roughly built,
and the pilothouse looks like a coffin. The net reels off
the bow.

We saw something coming off the cork line in front
of the bow of the boat. Then we saw an arm!

It was thirty-four to thirty-six degree water with ice
floes—small chunks of ice and sometimes huge bergs—
floating in it. People can only survive five minutes in
water this temperature.

We dropped the end ball, untied ourselves from our
net, and ran our boat over, and there, hanging on to her
cork line, was a kid, about seventeen years old. There
was no one else on the boat.

I hopped onto his boat and leaned over between the
uprights. The kid wasn't hypothermic, still pretty lively,

and came over as close to me as he could. I braced myself, grabbed him by the scruff of his collar, and pulled him up into the boat.

He told me his name was Sven Gildness. He'd made enough money fishing in the summers to buy his own boat and Alaskan permit. His mom made his dad promise to stay close, keep an eye on him, and see he didn't get into trouble. That day, his dad wasn't paying too much attention, and they'd gotten a ways apart.

I helped him get his net picked up, and because we were about ready to leave anyway, Dad hauled in our net too. I rode on Sven's boat to Cordova. He was cold, but capable, and I mainly stayed with him for moral support. On the way, he told me what had happened.

When we got to port, his mom and dad were waiting for him. He went up to meet them and tell them his story. He told them he'd leaned over between the uprights to get a bucket of water to freshen up the fish he'd hauled on board and to clean up the decks. Right at that moment, a boat came by, and its wake flipped him over the side. He hung there and hollered for help until Dad and I heard him.

His mom and dad came down to the dock and thanked us for saving their son. His mom then chewed his dad out for getting too far away from Sven, and they never heard the *real* story.

What had actually occurred was this. Sven leaned over the side, not between the uprights, and the rope to the bucket had slipped out of his hand. The bucket was plastic, and it floated. He leaned over with a gaff hook to reach it, and over the side he went! He swam around to the other side of his boat, where the fender was—often an old tire to keep boats from scraping sides—and threw the gaff hook into the boat. Still holding on to the rope of the bucket, which was full of water, he got up on top of the caprail, tried to scoozle around and get the bucket in, and fell in the water *again*.

By then, he was so cold, and no doubt more than a little scared, that he couldn't get back up into the boat.

So, he swam around and grabbed onto the rope coming off the bow that his net was attached to, hung on, and called for help. There were several other boats two or three net-lengths away—all within a quarter mile. But we were the closest, and downwind, and my dad happened to hear him.

Satisfied with the version of events Sven had told them, his folks were very grateful we had saved their son's life. His dad had recently bought an old cannery building, and he gave my dad free boat storage for the rest of that winter. Since this all happened some twenty-five years ago, it's probably okay if the truth comes out now.

After fishing and working here and there, including for National Marine Fisheries, Walt Receconi went back to school at the College of Optometry in Forest Grove, Oregon, where he met his wife. They both graduated with doctorates in Optometry and set up shop in Astoria, Oregon. They are both now retired.

"There was a round of laughter
from the passengers..."

Spend a Jolly Hour
on Our Astoria Trolley

Aletha and Bob Westerberg

When the trolley first came to town, we heard about it, thought it was a great thing, and sent a contribution to support the restoration work.

We didn't think too much about it until the spring of 2000 when I read an article in *The Daily Astorian* asking for volunteers to operate the trolley. That evening, I told my husband, Bob, that I wanted to get involved with the trolley.

He said, "That's great. You'll be able to give the spiel, no problem."

And I said, "I don't want to talk. I want to drive it!"

Well, he allowed I could probably do that, too.

We both took the classes, the tests, and the training runs and have been active with the Astoria River Front Trolley ever since. The smiles we encounter while running the trolley, both on the passengers' faces and on the faces of the people walking, riding, skating, and running along the River Walk, are part of the fun and rewards of taking time to serve the community.

People from all over come to Astoria, Oregon, and many of them ride the trolley. You can ride for $1 for a round trip or $2 all-day. Wave a bill, and the trolley will stop anywhere. Listening to the spiel and watching for the historical points mentioned are informative and fun. At the end of each trip, the trolley doesn't turn around.

The passengers get to flip the seats, and the trolley continues with the front end as the back end.

We have met lots of wonderful people—and many a cute dog—on the trolley. I remember one day, we had a total of five dogs on board at one time. They were all on their best behavior, and we had no incidents of any kind with them.

During the summer of 2004, a family of four from Colorado got on the trolley, but I could tell the mother, in particular, was irritated about something. It turned out they had missed the shuttle bus that would take them to Fort Clatsop, and that had been the whole point of the trip—following the trail of Lewis and Clark.

Bob and I consulted, and luckily, there was another trolley operator with us. We asked that driver to fill in for Bob while he delivered the family to Fort Clatsop. We promised to pick them up at 5:00 p.m. when the fort closed.

Well, I couldn't just take them back to their motel. First, I took them by the Japanese shell monument, where markers show the site of the only attack by the Japanese during World War II on a military installation on the U.S. mainland. Then, I drove them out to see the wreck of the Peter Iredale, a four-masted steel barque sailing vessel that ran ashore on October 25, 1906, on the coast en route to the Columbia River.

Their reaction was really something. They had never seen the ocean and hadn't thought they would get a chance on this trip since they didn't have a car. The teenagers were very excited about it and were quite talkative on the way back to their motel. We received a lovely thank you note from the family with an offer to show us around their area, if and when we were in ever in Colorado.

Another summer, a mom and three children happily climbed on the trolley. Bob noticed later, she was counting her money, and he heard her telling her children they didn't have enough to go to the Columbia River Maritime Museum.

He remembered we had Boarding Passes at home—museum members' one-time-only-use passes—so we arranged to get them to the family. On their return home, each member of the family wrote their own thank you note to us from Wyoming. The boys especially enjoyed the museum.

The Astoria River Front Trolley operator and conductor communicate with bell signals. Two bells from the conductor tell the operator he is clear to start. Two bells from the operator mean he heard the "start" bells. One bell from the conductor means stop at the next trolley stop, and the operator replies with one bell, indicating he heard the signal.

Bob and I were operating the trolley during a time when the inside bell on the west end was out of order. We agreed we would just use the outside bell. All was well and good, except the bells were not distinct separate rings.

About the third signal attempt, Bob turned around to me and asked, "Was that two bells?"

I replied over the microphone, "Yes, dear!"

There was a round of laughter from the passengers, and a lady standing next to me said, "You guys must be friends."

I replied, "No, we're married."

Then, red-faced, I felt I had to clarify that yes, we are, indeed, friends too!

Aletha and Bob Westerberg have three children, all married, and they have five grandchildren. They're involved in many local activities besides the Astoria River Front Trolley: the Maritime Museum, the annual Astoria Music Festival, and their church. Not only do they manage these affairs, but they also do the dishes. Aletha sings in the Cannon Beach Chorus, and Bob hosts Monday Morning Classics on KMUN, the local radio station.

"I have to secure our quarters," Nickolas informed her, taking her by the shoulders and setting her back from him.

"We're alone," she assured him.

Alone....Oh god... Swallowing hard, he forced himself away from her, pulled his Beretta from his shoulder holster and secured every room before returning. She was still standing in the living room where he had left her.

"Do you feel better now?" Talia asked with a small smile, kicking off her pumps.

Better? Not hardly. How could a woman removing her shoes be so damn sexy? She walked up to him and started unbuttoning his shirt. When he clamped his big hand over hers to still her action, she looked up into his eyes questioningly.

"Are you going to be able to sleep with that 'not-your-gun' in your pants?" she asked, glancing down at his tented suit slacks.

"Probably not. No." Even though he was in a serious hurt, he had to smile at her comment. His smile rapidly faded, however, when she resumed unbuttoning his shirt. "Talia, baby," he implored, wrapping his hand around her busy little fingers, "I have zero control, I don't want to run the risk of hurting you."

"I'm not as fragile as I look. I promise I won't break, Nickolas," she whispered, looking deeply into his eyes.

"Ah shit, baby," he groaned, sweeping her up and carrying her to the bedroom. He could no more stop himself now than he could stop breathing. He had to have her. She wrapped her arms around his thick neck and nuzzled against it as his long, determined strides carried her to the bed. He had to make it to the bed, damn it, he was *not* going to take her on the floor – or against the wall, or.....